MONTANA DOG SOLDIER

BROTHERHOOD PROTECTORS BOOK #6

ELLE JAMES

TWISTED PAGE INC.

MONTANA DOG SOLDIER

BROTHERHOOD PROTECTORS BOOK #6

New York Times & *USA Today*
Bestselling Author

ELLE JAMES

This story is dedicated to our military service dogs and their handlers, putting their lives on the line to save others.

Elle James

AUTHOR'S NOTE

Enjoy other military books by Elle James

Brotherhood Protectors Series
Montana SEAL (#1)
Bride Protector SEAL (#2)
Montana D-Force (#3)
Cowboy D-Force (#4)
Montana Ranger (#5)
Montana Dog Soldier (#6)
Montana SEAL Daddy (#7)
Montana Ranger's Wedding Vow (#8)
Montana SEAL Undercover Daddy (#9)
Cape Cod SEAL Rescue (#10)
Montana SEAL Friendly Fire (#11)
Montana SEAL's Mail-Order Bride (#12)
SEAL Justice (#13)
Ranger Creed (#14)
Delta Force Rescue (#15)
Montana Rescue (Sleeper SEAL)
Hot SEAL Salty Dog (SEALs in Paradise)
Hot SEAL Hawaiian Nights (SEALs in Paradise)
Hot SEAL Bachelor Party (SEALs in Paradise)
Brotherhood Protectors Vol 1

Visit ellejames.com for more titles and release dates

For hot cowboys, visit her alter ego Myla Jackson at
mylajackson.com
and join Elle James's Newsletter at
https://ellejames.com/contact/

CHAPTER 1

"Kujo, you're up." Bear stood at the door to the Black Hawk helicopter waving at him to step forward.

Joseph "Kujo" Kuntz stood, snapped the O-ring onto Six's harness and moved toward the door. He locked into the cable that would lower him and his dog to the ground into enemy territory.

Their mission: rescue two female soldiers being held by the Taliban in a remote Afghan village. Al Jazeera television had released videos of the women trussed up like animals, their faces bruised and battered, Taliban soldiers pressing rifles to their heads.

During his unit's briefing, the intel guys had replayed the video, displayed the satellite images of where they'd determined the women were being held and gone over and over the village layout.

Kujo's gut clenched every time he thought of the captives. He knew what Taliban men did to foreign women. If they didn't outright kill them, they tortured them until they wished they were dead. The looks in those two women's eyes were of beaten resolution. They were prepared to die. Perhaps praying for an end to the pain.

The video had the desired effect on the extraction team. They wanted to get in, rescue the hostages and put the hurt on the bastards who'd tortured the American women.

Yeah, he'd be just as determined to free them if they were male soldiers. Kujo didn't discriminate with his need to help any American in trouble. But he couldn't push aside an image of his sister or his mother in a similar situation. Those captured women could be someone's sister or even mother.

Rage roiled in his gut, churning, burning its way through his veins and firing up his adrenaline. He wanted to make those murdering, cowardly Taliban men pay for what they'd done.

Standing at the door of the aircraft, he channeled his rage into tightly strung control. First, his unit had to find the women and then safely get them out. That was his job. His, along with the aid of Six, his sable German Shepherd that had been trained to sniff out explosives.

The information the intelligence guys had received originated from one of their Afghan spies. After verifying the data via satellite, they'd formulated their plan. That's when Kujo and Six had been called in.

The commander had a bad feeling about the entire operation. The fact the women had been paraded on Al Jazeera led him to believe it was a setup, a potential trap. But they couldn't leave the women to the machinations of the Taliban. They wouldn't last much longer. If they were even still alive.

Thus, the quickly formed extraction team of available Delta Force and SEALs who'd performed similar operations over the past six months. The integrated team members had proven their abilities. They trusted every operator to have their backs.

The helicopter slowed and hovered behind the hill blocking the view of the village. They'd fast-rope to the ground and move in on foot.

In Kujo's case, he and Six would be lowered to the ground by cable. Once they were there, they'd slip into the village, Six taking point to sniff out the danger of IEDs or other types of explosives the enemy might have set out to welcome their insertion.

Kujo briefly rested his hand on Six's head. The dog nuzzled it, and then waited patiently for their cue to step out.

"Go!" Bear said.

Kujo grabbed Six's harness, stepped out the door of the aircraft and dangled from the cable as they were quickly lowered to the ground.

Six didn't whine. He hung in his harness beside Kujo, his gaze fixed on the darkness below.

The dog had been whelped in Germany and spent the first year of his life there. He still responded to many German commands.

When he had been assigned to Kujo for training in the United States at Lackland Air Force Base, Kujo had called him by the last number of the tattoo on his left ear, ß826. The number just happened to coincide with the number of dogs Kujo had worked with in his career with the Army. He'd learned through the loss of the first five animals not to get too attached. They belonged to the Army.

His first dog, Fritz, had been a Belgian Malinois. He'd saved countless lives before he'd stepped on an IED and died in Kujo's arms. His second and third dogs had been German Shepherds whelped in the United States by a trusted breeder. They'd been retired after they grew skittish over the sounds of explosions.

The fourth, another Malinois, had developed a tumor in her face and had to be euthanized. The fifth, Rambo, had been a very smart black Labrador who'd saved many lives sniffing out IEDs, but he'd been too close to an explosion and lost his hearing. A retired Brigadier General and his wife in Colorado Springs had adopted Rambo and given him a great retirement home.

For five intensive months of training, Kujo had worked with Six, getting him ready to deploy. The animal had responded quickly, learning what he needed to know to help save lives in war-torn countries.

As soon as Kujo's boots touched ground, he unclipped his harness from the cable, reached for the O-ring, and released Six. The dog knew his mission and took off.

Other members of the team were already on the ground, having rappelled from the aircraft.

The Black Hawk lifted and swung away from them. The pilot would be far enough away to be out of range of RPGs and small arms fire, but the help would be quick to respond should the team radio for extraction.

Six led them over the hill and up to the village, sniffing his way through brush and the rocky terrain. So far, so good.

Perhaps, too good. No resistance, no guards perched on the rooftop.

The hairs on the back of Kujo's neck rose.

The team's weapons were fixed with sound suppression. Moving through a village, they relied heavily on stealth. For each mission, they strove to get in and get out, undetected. Their sound-suppressed weapons allowed them to fire a shot in one room of a building without being heard from another.

Kujo carried an HK MP7A1 submachine gun. The lightweight weapon allowed him to be more mobile and deadly, without announcing to the world or the village he was there.

As they approached the village, Kujo and Six moved ahead of the team. In the dead of night when most people slept, nothing moved but the team.

They paused just outside the village in a jumble of large boulders and scanned the buildings using night vision goggles, or NVGs, searching for heat signatures —the shadowy, green silhouettes of enemy soldiers perched on rooftops.

"Cover me," Kujo said.

"Gotcha," Bear replied into his headset. "Go."

Kujo sent Six forward several feet before he followed, hunkering close to the earth, moving swiftly toward the stick and mud wall surrounding the village. As soon as he arrived, he waited, providing cover for the others as they traveled the same path cleared by Six.

Bear knelt at the base of the barrier.

Kujo stepped onto his back and pulled himself up to the top of the wall and scanned the immediate surroundings through his NVGs. When he was certain the area was clear of enemy personnel, he motioned for Six to follow. Six leaped up on Bear's back and over the wall, dropped to the ground below and went to work.

Kujo slipped to the ground behind him and directed the dog down an alley between buildings toward their target. According to the satellite images in their briefing, the intel folks believed the women were being held in the largest of the mud and brick structures at the back of the village where it hugged the base of a rocky cliff.

At one corner, Six paused and waited for his handler to catch up.

Kujo stopped beside the dog, and sneaked a peek around the corner. Nothing moved. The town was too quiet. His gut tightened. He spotted the target location. "Building in sight."

"We'll cover," Bear said. "When you're ready, go"

"Roger," Kujo whispered, careful not to give away his position. To his partner, he gave the signal for the animal to move forward, nose to the ground, quietly sniffing, doing the job he'd been trained to do, search for explosives ahead of the humans.

Kujo could see the green outline of Six as the dog rounded the corner, his nose to the ground.

First into the village, members of the dog handling team had to be on their toes, whether two or four-legged. Their job was to warn the others of potential explosive hazards.

Kujo and Six had graduated top of their class during concentrated training at Joint Base Lackland in San Antonio. They'd received additional Tactical Explosive Detection (TED) training in southern Afghanistan before they'd been attached to the Delta Force unit where Kujo, a trained Delta Force soldier, reconnected with a couple of men he'd served with, Bear and Duke, prior to being trained as a dog handler.

He was glad to be back among men who'd shared some of the most intense missions of their lives. They'd survived because of their attention to detail, dogged preparation and dedication to teamwork, and all of them had come back alive.

Six moved through the narrow walkways between the buildings. Every so often, he would return to Kujo for instruction, and Kujo would send him back out.

They worked their way toward the target, coming to a halt twenty feet short, across the road and at the edge of a squat structure. Six returned to Kujo's side and sat, staring ahead, his head raised, ears perked high, ready and alert.

Bear moved in behind Kujo and waited for the rest of the small team to catch up.

"Too quiet," Kujo stated, his voice soft, barely enough to register on a radio. "Be alert."

Bear nodded, his face grim. He glanced back at the team. "Ready?"

Everyone nodded.

Three men took positions on either side of the alleyway to provide cover.

Kujo gave the signal for Six to search for explosives.

The dog set out in the dark, moonless night, with nothing but starlight to guide him.

Kujo watched, waiting for Six to indicate the presence of explosives.

A trickle of sweat slipped down the side of his neck. The earth retained much of the heat from the oven-baking, one-hundred-twenty-degree temperature of the day. Loaded with weapons, his vest and steel plate, Kujo carried an additional fifty pounds of gear.

A minute later, Six returned, tail wagging, anxious to please.

Kujo patted his head. "Let's go."

Kujo, Bear and Duke took the lead, with the others as backup. They approached the building at an angle, running in a low crouch toward the entrance.

Six arrived at the door first and sniffed the ground and doorframe, but he didn't sit, which would have indicated the presence of explosives.

While Bear and Duke flattened their bodies against the side of the building, Kujo pushed the door. It didn't move. He pulled a Ka-Bar knife from the scabbard on his side and slid it between the door and the frame, applied a little force and the door opened.

He toed it open and stepped aside. If someone had been on the other side, he wouldn't have an immediate target.

Kujo signaled to Six. The dog trotted through the entrance.

Figuring Six would have growled or tensed if someone had been inside, Kujo concluded the room was unoccupied and entered behind the dog, keeping low, and shifting quickly out of the doorframe.

Six made a quick survey of the room, nose to the ground, and headed for a hallway.

"Clear," Kujo whispered into his headset.

Six continued his search, one room at a time.

Bear and Duke followed Kujo down the hallway. The rooms were empty except for discarded cardboard boxes and empty cans and bottles. A wad of blankets was piled in the corner. Kujo nudged the blankets, praying he wouldn't find the dead bodies of the women beneath. He released the breath he'd been holding when he realized they were only rags.

He moved on, bounding past Duke to check the third room along the hallway, and then moved on to the doorway at the end.

Six was already there, sniffing at the gap beneath the door. He glanced up at Kujo and then sat.

Holy hell. Kujo's gut clenched.

The dog had identified the scent of explosives. The door wasn't closed all the way; it hung open a good four inches, and the room beyond was shrouded in darkness.

Kujo glanced back at Bear and Duke as they exited the rooms they'd cleared and waited for further instruction.

"We have a problem," Kujo said, hoping the others would hear his softly spoken words.

He didn't have to spell out the problem. Bear and Duke would deduce the issue, seeing Six sitting on his haunches, proud of his find and awaiting his next command.

Without a doubt, some kind of explosive device awaited the team behind that half-opened door. The only question remaining was whether the women were also inside the room.

A noise came from the darkness, sounding like a muffled sob.

Kujo's initial instinct was to step forward, toward the sound. He reached out, but paused before pushing open the door. If it were wired to the explosives, he would end up killing the women, the dog and himself. Instead, he pulled a shiny piece of metal from his pocket and squatted beside the door. Holding the metal mirror in his hand, he pushed his hand through the opening and angled the mirror so that he could see what was inside.

A small glimmer of light glowed in a far corner. Using the mirror's reflection, Kujo scanned the room until he found what he was looking for.

His hand froze and a lead weight settled in the pit of his gut. The women were there, and they were alive. But they wouldn't be for long.

Gagged and bound together, they were also equipped with vests of explosives of the kind suicide bombers wore beneath their robes.

Anger rose in Kujo's chest. The door wasn't rigged. The women were.

He slowly pushed the door wider but didn't enter. Instead, he slid his NVGs up onto his helmet and beamed a tiny flashlight toward the female soldiers.

The women blinked their swollen eyelids open and spotted him. Their eyes rounded, and they started shaking their heads, grunting through the wads of cloth in their mouths.

His gut told him not to enter the room, so he hesitated and motioned for Six to back away from the door. He studied the explosives from a distance, but he couldn't locate the detonator from where he stood. About the time he considered entering, a blinding flash burst around him and the world exploded.

The half-open door was blasted off its hinges and slammed into Kujo, knocking him off his feet. He landed on his back, his ears ringing, pain knifing through his knee and his head, his chest feeling as though a weight pressed down on his ribs. The air quickly filled with dust. If he could have breathed, he was sure he'd have choked.

Before he completely lost consciousness, he felt something sharp dig into his arm, and then he was being dragged across rubble. Before he could glance sideways at his rescuer, darkness closed in, burying him in a bottomless abyss.

CHAPTER 2

THREE YEARS LATER...

KUJO STOOD on the front porch of the log cabin, staring out at the snow-capped Rockies and scratching the beard he hadn't bothered to shave since he'd been medically boarded out of the Army three years before.

Why bother? He wasn't wearing the uniform, he didn't have a job, and he didn't even have to get out of bed in the morning.

He walked to the end of the deck and stretched in the cool mountain air. Though he'd been out of the military for a few years, he still worked out to keep his knee from stiffening. The operation to replace the torn ligaments had left him with a limp, but he refused to be a burden on anyone. So, every morning, he got his ass out of the bed and worked through the pain until he could walk. He was recovered enough he could even run again. But his knee wasn't the same, nor was his head.

Traumatic Brain Injury sucked. For the first few months after the explosion, he'd had blinding headaches at least once a week, and sometimes more. As time had passed, the headaches had eased and he was getting around better. He'd moved from his apartment outside Ft. Bragg, North Carolina to the mountains of Colorado to get away from the crowds and his old buddies, who'd drop in to cheer him up while they felt sorry for his suffering.

God, he hated pity. So, he wasn't in the military any more. So the fuck what. He had enough money coming in from his disability to survive. Barely. He'd been fortunate to rent this log cabin in the woods, too far off the beaten path to appeal to tourists. Without internet or cell phone coverage, not many city folk wanted to stay there. He'd worked a deal with the aging owner to live there at a very low rent as long as he fixed up the place.

He'd lived up to his end of the bargain and repaired everything that needed it, to the point he had nothing left to do. Now, he considered building a shed behind the cabin to house a four-wheeler he kept under a lean-to. He'd even dressed in a pair of jeans without holes and put on his least offensive boots for the trip into town in his old pickup.

About to step off the porch, he spotted a shiny, black four-wheel-drive Jeep climbing the rutted road up to the cabin.

Kujo frowned. He liked his privacy. When people wandered near, he gave them the stink-eye and told them they were trespassing on private property. If the look and the verbal warning didn't work, his glare, thick beard, shaggy hair and scarred face were threatening enough to scare them off.

Standing with his arms crossed over his chest, he frowned fiercely and waited for the Jeep to come to a standstill in front of the cabin. He hoped the people would get the hell out of there quickly. He had work to do, and he wouldn't leave the cabin while strangers wandered around the property.

As soon as the Jeep came to a halt, two men climbed out.

Kujo's frown deepened. The sunlight bounced off the windshield, blinding him. All he could tell was that the men were big, with broad shoulders and thick thighs. They wore leather jackets and cowboy hats, and carried themselves like men with a purpose.

"You've come far enough," he said, squinting against the glare. "You're trespassing. If you're lost, head back the way you came."

The men drew closer, moving out of the glare from the Jeep's windshield. They tipped their heads to stare up at where he stood on the porch.

"Kujo?" one of the men said in a familiar baritone. "Is that you?"

"Shit, dude, what the hell have you done to yourself?" the other man said.

A flood of emotions washed over Kujo. No one had called him Kujo since he'd left his unit in Afghanistan, extracted from the Afghan village on Bear's back. From there, he'd been transported to the nearest field hospital where they'd stabilized him then shipped him to the rear and out of the area of operations to the hospital in Landstuhl, Germany. Doctors had relieved the pressure on his brain and monitored him there for a couple days, and then evacuated him stateside to Walter Reed. All the while, he hadn't awakened. Not until the swelling subsided had he surfaced from the darkness that had claimed him. He hadn't remembered the explosion, and he barely remembered his name.

Two weeks had passed since the operation in Afghanistan before he learned of the deaths of the women. The explosives had been remotely detonated.

Someone had to remind him that he'd been a dog handler. He'd become distraught, asking about Six and the other members of the team.

Thankfully, Bear, Duke and the others had survived. If not for the door and the walls deflecting most the explosion, they all could have died. Aside from the deaths of the females who'd been rigged with the demolitions, Kujo was the only one seriously injured. Even Six had only minor shrapnel wounds. He'd been treated and assigned a new handler.

After his knee operation and physical therapy, Kujo had seen the writing on the wall. He'd never get back to the same physical condition he'd been in before the explosion. And, because of the TBI, the Army didn't want to risk putting him back in dangerous situations where others would rely on his mental acuity.

Thus, he'd lost his military family, his dog and his

career in one fell swoop. By the time his physical therapy was complete, he had nothing left of his former life. Living near Ft. Bragg had only reminded him of all he'd lost. So, he'd packed his duffel bag, sold his furniture and left.

He'd driven all the way to Colorado before he stopped, exhausted, his knee hurting and his head aching. Up in the mountains, he felt like he could breathe again, away from his memories.

Until now.

Standing before him, on the mountain he'd come to think of as his own, were two of the best friends a man could have. Two men who had risked their lives for him on multiple occasions. He should have been happy to see them. For a moment, he felt that old joy of seeing his long-lost friends, but just as quickly the joy was gone. They were part of what he was trying so hard to forget.

"Why are you here?" he demanded, his voice brusque.

Bear's jaw hardened. "Because we care."

"Do you know how hard it was to track you down?" Duke grunted. "If it weren't for the man at the hardware store in town, we might never have found you up here."

Kujo shrugged. "I like my privacy."

Bear shook his head. "We all like our privacy, but this takes it to an entirely new level."

Kujo wasn't much for talking. "Again, why are you here?"

"We got word from your former trainer at Lackland that Six is there. He was injured in an IED explosion and has been retired from active duty," Bear said.

"He's up for adoption," Duke finished.

Kujo's gut twisted. He'd spent the past three years trying to remember the details of what happened on his last mission, and to forget about the people and the dog he'd more or less lost. He couldn't go through that again. Forcing a nonchalance he didn't feel, he shrugged again. "So?"

Bear glanced at Duke and back to Kujo. "We thought you'd want to know and that you might consider taking him."

Something inside Kujo's heart pinched so tightly that, for a moment, he thought he might be having an attack. He pressed a hand to his chest in an effort to relieve the pressure. "He was a good dog. Why wouldn't he find a good home?"

"He's been available for months. He's had two foster families take him, but they couldn't handle him and returned him. Because of his injury, he limps. No one else has stepped forward to take him. Your former trainer contacted us, thinking you might want him."

"No." Kujo turned and walked away. "That part of my life is over."

"Yeah, but here's the deal," Duke called after him. "If you don't take him, he's scheduled to be put down in three days."

Kujo whipped around. "Put down?"

Duke nodded. "He's on death row. No one wants him, and you're his last hope."

"Why don't you take him?" Kujo shot back at his former teammates.

Duke shrugged. "We don't know how to handle him.

He's got issues. Since you left the service, he's been through four different handlers and been injured. He's punchy. The dog needs a stable influence."

Bear squinted up at him. "Your trainer thinks he doesn't trust anyone. No one sticks around."

Kujo grimaced. It wasn't like he'd wanted to leave Six. The dog belonged to Uncle Sam. Just like Kujo once had. The powers that be in the military had the say regarding where a soldier or a war dog went.

The Army had dropped Kujo. Now they wanted to drop Six.

His gut clenched, and his throat tightened. "I can't," he said.

Bear raised his brows. "So, you're willing to let him die?"

No! But he couldn't put his heart into another dog. The pain of loss had taken a toll on Kujo.

"Look, think about it." Bear glanced around at the cabin. "In the meantime, are you going to invite us in?"

With all his thoughts focused on Six, Kujo stared at Bear for a moment until his words sank in. Slowly, he nodded. "It's nice outside. You want to have a seat on the porch? I'd offer you a beer, but I'm all out. How's coffee."

"That would be good," Bear agreed and stepped up onto the porch.

"I'll take a cup, too," Duke said, climbing up the steps. He walked to the end of the porch and stared down at the valley surrounded by snow-capped peaks. "What a view. I can see why you like it here."

Kujo's gaze followed Duke's. He'd felt the peace as

18

soon as he'd driven into the valley and up to the cabin. No other place had that effect on him at a time when he needed to calm the anger and still his jumbled thoughts.

"I'll be back."

He disappeared into the house, a dull ache forming at the base of his skull. He hadn't seen familiar faces in so long, he wasn't sure how he felt. On one hand, he was glad to see Bear and Duke. They'd been as close, if not closer, than any blood brothers could be. Yet, they brought with them all the memories he'd tried too hard to forget.

Kujo went through the motions of making coffee, while getting his shit together. A few minutes later, he emerged from the house.

"I think Hank would agree," Bear was saying.

"Me, too." Duke said. "Let's do it."

The two men had taken seats on the only two seats on the porch—rocking chairs faded from the weather, but sturdy and comfortable.

As Kujo stepped out onto the deck, carrying two steaming mugs he asked, "Do what?" He handed a mug to each of his Delta Force comrades, and then leaned against the rail, folding his arms over his chest. By their cagey looks, they'd been discussing him.

Bear sipped the hot brew then glanced up at Kujo. "What are you doing up here in the mountains?"

Kujo stiffened. Where was Bear going with his question? "I've been working on this cabin."

Bear studied the structure for a moment. "I take it you don't have a real job."

Kujo's back stiffened. "I take my work seriously."

"The place looks great. How much acreage do you own with the cabin?"

Kujo's teeth ground together. "I don't own the cabin."

Duke's brows rose. "You're working on a cabin you don't own?"

"Yeah." Kujo frowned. "So?"

"What do you do for a living?"

"I have my medical retirement from the Army." He pushed away from the rail, his eyes narrowing. "Why do you ask?"

Bear shot a glance at Duke. "We have a proposition for you."

Kujo turned away and stared out at the mountains, willing the craggy peaks to bring him the peace he'd always expected from them. "Not interested."

"At least hear us out before you decide," Duke said. "Bear and I are out of the Army, too. We weren't sure what kind of work we could do after being Delta Force. The transition was rough."

"Until Hank Patterson offered us a job," Bear added.

Kujo half-turned. "Who the hell is Hank Patterson?"

Bear grinned. "A SEAL who left the Navy to help his father on his ranch in Montana."

Kujo frowned. "I don't know anything about ranching."

Bear arched an eyebrow. "I'm not saying you'll be ranching."

Duke blew on the coffee and took another sip. "Hank set up an organization in the foothills of the Crazy Mountains of Montana."

Kujo shook his head. "I'm not interested in being a survivalist or prepper, or whatever they're calling them now."

Duke grinned. "No, it's nothing like that. He started a service called Brotherhood Protectors. He hires the best of the best of former active duty military."

"SEALs, Marines, D-Force," Bear continued. "We provide protective services to clients who need them."

"He's given more than a few former fighters the chance to make a difference outside of the military." Bear tipped his head toward Duke. "We both work for Brotherhood Protectors."

"What does this have to do with me?"

Bear leveled his gaze on Kujo. "We think you'd be a good fit for the team."

Well, I don't. They don't know me anymore. Still, he couldn't help asking, "Why me?"

"For one," Bear said, "we don't have any dog handlers among us. I believe there's a need for one."

"I don't have a dog," Kujo reminded them.

"You don't have one *now*," Duke corrected.

Kujo straightened. "I'm not going to adopt Six."

Duke's lips thinned. "That dog is a highly decorated hero, just like you. I think he could be of use to the organization."

"But he needs someone who can handle him," Bear added.

Duke nodded. "He needs you."

Bear leveled a stare at Kujo. "*We* need you."

Kujo held up his hands. "I'm not interested."

"What do you have holding you here?" Bear asked.

"I have a life here," Kujo insisted.

"Are you happy?" Duke asked.

"Who says you have to be happy?" Kujo turned away. His thoughts tumbled, his stomach roiled and his head pounded. "I just want to be left alone"

"Really?" A hand descended on his shoulder. Bear stood beside him. "You used to like to hang with the team. Have a beer. Work out with the guys. Do you really like being here? Alone?"

That hollowness he'd felt since he'd left the service had intensified. Three years on his own and all the forgetting and pushing memories to the back of his mind meant nothing. Everything seemed to flow back into his thoughts, into his head.

Memories of his buddies sitting around his apartment, drinking beer and watching football, filled his mind. The times they stood at the door to the helicopter, adrenaline flowing, ready to punch out and do their jobs in an enemy-infested landscape. Sharing the camaraderie only men who'd faced death and survived could relate to.

The hand on his shoulder seemed to burn through his shirt, the heat penetrating to that cold hard organ that used to be his heart.

Bear tucked a business card into Kujo's shirt pocket. "Think about it, will ya?" he said. "We need men like you."

And Kujo needed *them*.

The thought surfaced before he could shove it to the far reaches of his consciousness.

"And Six needs you," Duke said. "Please, don't let him become yet another casualty to a thankless war."

Out of the corner of his gaze, Kujo watched Bear step down from the porch.

His former teammate said, "You have a lot to think about, so, we'll be going now. If you want to join us for a beer, you can find us in town until eleven o'clock tomorrow when we check out of our hotel."

Duke and Bear climbed into the Jeep and left, kicking up a trail of dust in their wake.

Kujo followed the vehicle's progress until it disappeared through the trees.

Up until that moment, he thought he'd been holding his own pretty well and had come to grips with his new normal.

The visit from his old teammates dispelled that fallacy. As the dust settled on the mountain road, Kujo didn't think he could feel more alone in the world. An awful, empty feeling threatened to overwhelm him. The longer he stood there, the tighter his gut clenched.

Ten minutes later, he entered the cabin and trimmed the shaggy beard, and then shaved his face clean. He packed his duffel bag with everything he'd brought with him when he'd moved into the cabin.

He didn't think too much, just followed his gut, moving like an automaton, not willing to overthink the situation—afraid that if he did, he'd completely fall apart.

Maybe he and Six could provide some value to Hank Patterson's Brotherhood Protectors...if the organization needed two broken-down soldiers. All he knew was Six needed him. Kujo hadn't been able to save the female soldiers, but he could do something about saving the dog soldier.

CHAPTER 3

M<small>OLLY</small> G<small>REENBRIAR</small> <small>GOOSED</small> the throttle on the ATV, sending it bumping over the rocky road up into the hills beyond the small town of Eagle Rock. With only a few minutes of instruction from the man she'd rented the vehicle from, she wasn't as confident as she'd like to be handling the four-wheeler on the dangerous mountain roads and trails. She wasn't in a hurry to get up to the top, nor was she in a hurry to go plunging off a cliff.

Taking the ascent slowly, she eased up the hill, keeping her gaze peeled for potential threats from man or beast. She was on a mission and had no intention of failing because she hadn't taken sufficient precautions.

As she neared the top of a ridge, she slowed to a stop, switched off the engine, dismounted and pulled off her helmet. As she stared out across the Crazy Mountains of Western Montana, she couldn't help feeling she was as close to Heaven as any mortal could be. If she weren't working, she'd be exploring these mountains, anyway. Unfortunately, though the scenery was beautiful and the mountains were breathtaking, they could potentially be harboring a deadly faction bent on harming innocent people.

She wrestled the drone out of the basket on the back of the four-wheeler and laid the parts on the ground. Then kneeling beside them on the rocky terrain, she assembled the pieces and adjusted the settings. She'd practiced with the device with the help of an instructor back in D.C., but flying it solo was an entirely different undertaking.

She didn't have the backup of the instructor. If she lost control of the drone and crashed it into the side of a cliff, she'd have a lot of explaining to do to her boss back at FBI Headquarters in DC. She straightened with the controls in her hands.

With her first opportunity to prove herself in the field, failure wasn't an option. She'd begged her boss, Pete Ralston, to let her come out to the Crazy Mountains, chasing a lead on a terrorist training camp in the vicinity of Eagle Rock.

A tip from one of the FBI computer gurus had landed on her desk at headquarters, indicating a growing concern over what appeared to be tactical training activities underway by individuals connected to some of the most dangerous ISIS sympathizers on US soil.

After investigating the lead, Molly had studied satellite photos of the area, spotting certain anomalies that indicated a suspicious concentration of people in the mountains, and they appeared to be conducting some sort of military-style maneuvers. The images set off alarm bells in Molly's mind, so she presented her findings to her boss. Unfortunately, she'd approached him at the same time a terrorist had plowed a truck into a crowd of tourists near the front of the White House. Her boss hadn't had time to review her research.

So sure of her findings, she'd asked to go to Montana to investigate with boots on the ground.

At first her boss had told her no. She didn't have experience as a field agent. He'd been buried in responding to calls from the press and House and Senate committees about the White House incident, as well as bombarded by the POTUS and his staff to give them answers about the man responsible for the White House incident.

In a weak moment, her boss had approved her assignment and the use of a drone for surveillance. "Strictly surveillance," he'd warned. "You are not to engage without backup. Get the information and get it back to me."

Thrilled, Molly had rushed home to pack a bag. Not only would it be her first time in the field, it would get her out of DC and away from everything that reminded her of Scott and the shambles of their failed relationship.

Molly adjusted the controls, and the drone lifted off the ground, hovered twenty feet in the air and then rose, moving out across a valley.

The time was long past for her to leave DC. When she completed this assignment, she'd put in for a transfer to a field office, anywhere but in the nation's capital, far enough away from Scott and his new fiancé that she'd never run into them again.

When he'd moved out of their apartment, he'd said he needed time to think. What he'd really meant to say was that he'd fallen in love with someone else. Within a month of moving out, he'd proposed to one of the secretaries from an office several doors down from where he and Molly worked.

Yes, Molly had been hurt when he'd left. But not devastated. She'd been more humiliated than anything else. As was the usual case for the spurned woman, she hadn't seen it coming. They'd been living together for over a year. Sex had become routine, and not anything to write home about. In fact, for the last two months they'd lived together, Scott had worked later and later. By the time he'd come home, Molly was asleep.

Molly shook her head over her own stupidity. In a convoluted way, losing Scott had led her here to this remote mountain pass. If she hadn't thrown herself into work, she might have missed seeing the clues. So, her personal life was in shambles. So the hell what? She'd prove herself ready for fieldwork and never look back.

The drone whirred across the valley, bringing Molly back to the present. She maneuvered it lower, while she scanned the digital screen, studying the terrain through the drone's camera.

She'd established herself in the nearby town as a nature and history enthusiast in Eagle Rock to film footage of the Crazy Mountains for a documentary she was working on.

She'd met with the local sheriff's department and

representatives from the forestry commission and the national parks, as well as the county commission, to study the local land survey maps. She'd needed a better understanding of who owned the land up to the edges of the national parks and forests, and where she could legally ride the four-wheel-drive ATV she'd rented.

All the research and preparations had taken a few days, but finally, she was out in the mountains, armed with her GPS, the drone, a backpack of survival gear and her personal 9-millimeter pistol. She wasn't supposed to engage, but she was prepared. Not only did she have to worry about being discovered by terrorists, she had to be bear aware. She was in grizzly country, and the area was also known for the wolves that had been reintroduced to the region.

Molly hoped the pistol was enough. She'd considered bringing a rifle as well. Perhaps she needed something even more powerful to stop a grizzly in its tracks.

At the moment, she was alone on a hilltop. The only wildlife she'd noticed was the occasional bird flying overheard.

She maneuvered the drone lower, toward a small river burbling through the valley. Molly had a lot of territory to cover. If there was a training site in the mountains, the people conducting and attending would have to be able to get into the area.

Molly was armed with topographical maps indicating all roads, paved and dirt, leading into the mountains along with the elevations and landmarks. As vast as the range was, she might be searching for a needle in a haystack. She had to think like the people leading the effort to train terrorists on US soil. She had to find where they had moved their encampment between multiple satellite images.

The FBI's computer guru had been unable to trace the tip to the source. Molly figured it had to be someone in the Eagle Rock area since the tip had specifically mentioned the mountains west of the small town.

Part of her investigation would be to find her informant. In the meantime, she'd do her best to locate the training site using the drone.

She'd drawn quadrants on the maps she'd acquired, and set about using the drone to scan each for any signs of suspicious activities.

Today was her first official trek into the mountains after the few days of preparation. The weather had been sunshine and blue skies all week, with the glorious backdrop of snow-capped peaks. This morning had been no different. But as soon as she rode her four-wheeler up the trail into the hills on the outskirts of Eagle Rock, clouds had slipped in from the west, blocking out the cheerful sunshine.

Molly didn't let it slow her down. She kept watch on the weather situation, knowing the trail would become treacherous should it start raining or, God forbid, snowing.

She'd positioned the drone at the western end of the valley and moved it slowly over the terrain, heading east toward the western fence line, surrounding land belonging to Bert Daniels, a cattle rancher who'd inherited his property from a long line of Daniels'. Molly had yet to meet the man, but she planned on talking to as many of the locals as possible, as casually as she could, without giving away her real purpose for coming to Eagle Rock.

Her first pass through the valley yielded nothing out of the ordinary. The only movement had been from a herd of antelope grazing on the grasses near the river. She'd observed no signs of manmade structures or roads leading in or out that appeared to have been heavily travelled.

She retrieved the drone and drove farther south along a narrow road that could have been an old mining road, or a logging road placed there years ago by a logging company when they'd still been allowed to harvest trees from the national forest. She took up a position at the top of another ridge and turned the key, killing the engine.

A noise behind her made her spin around. An animal burst from the tree line and barreled toward her.

Molly tensed and reached for her weapon. She'd been warned to be on the lookout for wolves and bear. At first, she thought wolf, but the animal didn't have the thick fur of a wolf. It appeared to be a German Shepherd. What a German Shepherd was doing out in these wild hills was another question.

If the animal was feral, it could be as dangerous as a wolf. As she watched, it bounded toward her, its gait not as graceful as most dogs. When it slowed, it settled into a limping trot.

Molly raised her weapon, not willing to take chances that the dog was friendly. If it growled or bared its teeth, she'd shoot first, ask questions later.

When the animal was within ten feet of Molly, she called out. "Sit!"

The German Shepherd stopped in its tracks and sat.

Molly frowned. "Are you a good dog or a bad dog?" she said aloud.

The shepherd's tail swished back and forth in the dirt.

"Here, boy," she said, calling it closer. Molly held the pistol in one hand and extended her other hand with her fingers curled under for the dog to sniff—and it did.

A long pink tongue snaked out and licked her hand.

"Ah, you're just a big sweetie." Molly holstered her weapon beneath her jacket, squatted on her haunches and ruffled the dog's neck, scratching behind his ears. "What are you doing out this far? Are you lost?" She looked the animal over. He appeared to be in good health, except for a scar on his leg and being a little thin. Had another animal attacked him? The wound appeared to be an old one. Though the hair had not grown back over the wound, it had healed long ago, the scar gray instead of the pink of a newer injury.

"What about a collar?" Molly felt around his neck and found a thick, leather band but no identification tag. However, he had a tattoo in his ear, ß826. "No dog tags but a tattoo? Are you a working dog, perhaps? Where's your master?"

As if in answer to her question, a movement caught her attention, and a man emerged from the same direction the dog had come. He wore jeans and hiking boots. A short-sleeved, black T-shirt stretched over impossibly broad shoulders, and his biceps bulged beneath the sleeves' hems.

Shaggy dark hair and dark stubble shadowing his chin gave him the appearance of a rugged mountain man, or a badass biker dude.

Molly caught her breath.

"Six," he said in one short, sharp command.

The dog leaped to his feet, ran back to the man and sat at his feet, looking up, ready to execute the next command.

His master stared at Molly through narrowed eyes.

She straightened, though standing up didn't make her feel any more in charge. The man towered over her. He could take her down with one hand tied behind his back. He could easily snap her neck in one twist.

Was he one of the people she'd come to Montana to find? A shiver rippled down the back of her neck. Unwilling to show even a small sign of fear, Molly squared her shoulders and tilted up her chin. "Is this your dog?"

He nodded. "He is. I hope he didn't scare you."

Her chin lifted a fraction more. "Not at all. I just wondered what he was doing out here, all alone."

His eyes narrowed even more, giving him a dark and dangerous look. "I could ask you the same."

"I'm enjoying the scenery," she stalled.

He held out a hand. "I'm Joe."

She hesitated before taking his hand. "Just Joe?" she challenged, narrowing her own eyes.

"Just Joe." He cocked a brow and waited for her to reciprocate. "And you are?"

"Molly," she said, not giving any more than he'd given. If he wanted his surname to remain anonymous, so be it. She could play the same game. A man like him would be easily recognized in town.

His lips twitched, and the slight crinkling at the corner of his eyes gave away his humor. "Just Molly?"

She gave the barest of nods, and then glanced down at the dog. "Yours?"

The little bit of laughter in his face died and a mask slid in its place. "Yeah."

"He's beautiful and friendly."

A frown pulled his brows together. "You touched him?"

Molly nodded. "Yes. Is it a crime?"

"Do you always pet strange dogs?"

"Only ones who let me."

"Ever consider they might bite?"

Oh, she'd considered it. She'd almost shot the poor animal. "Yes. But he sat when I told him to, so I figured he had some manners." *Unlike his master.*

"Did you ever consider their owners might not want you to pet them?"

Her brows shot up. "You don't want me to pet your dog?"

He shrugged. "Six is a highly trained dog. In order to keep control over him, it's best for only one person to give him commands."

She raised her hands in surrender, anger pushing to the surface. "Excuse me. The dog didn't come to me with instructions. But he did come to me." Molly crossed her arms over her chest. "And what the hell kind of name is Six?"

"None of your business," he muttered. "Why are you out in the mountains alone?" He looked over her shoulder at the four-wheeler and the drone.

Molly stood taller, as if in an attempt to block his view of her equipment. "None of your business."

He gave a curt nod and turned his attention to the dog. "Six, come." Without another word to her, the man departed, his dog trotting alongside. Both had a bit of a hitch in their gaits, both on the same side, as if they had received matching injuries.

For a long moment, Molly stared after them. Then she shook her head, climbed on her ATV and drove along the ridge in the opposite direction as the man had gone.

Rude. The man was completely rude.

On the other hand, the dog was sweet and well-mannered. "Joe" could learn a thing or two from his dog.

Following the directions to the locations she'd programmed into her GPS, she drove down an old mining trail into another valley and up to the top of the next ridge where she stopped, got out the drone and surveyed the next valley that featured a sheer rock wall lined with caves.

She fought to push the odious man to the back of her mind, but she couldn't help looking around every so often, as if half-expecting Just Joe to appear again.

Again, she sent the drone into the air, maneuvering it

slowly across the valley, pausing it in front of the caves to give her a chance to peek inside. She had her head down and was staring at the video imaging when a loud bang rang out, echoing off the hillsides. The view on the screen jerked to the side, bounced then began to spin.

Molly looked across the valley to the last location she'd sent the drone. The device had disappeared altogether and no amount of fiddling with the joystick brought it up again. Her drone was down, and based on the sound prefacing its crash, someone could have used it as target practice.

"Damn." Over a thousand dollars' worth of electronics had just crashed into the valley below.

Though she wasn't supposed to make contact, Molly had to know if a terrorist or a redneck poacher had shot down the drone.

She tucked the controls into her jacket, and pushed the four-wheeler into the bushes. Then she headed down the trail into the valley, hugging the shadows.

If the shooter were willing to take down a drone out in the middle of nowhere, would he also be willing to shoot a living, breathing human? Even if that person wasn't part of the terrorist training camp, he might not want to be caught shooting down an expensive piece of machinery. He might shoot at the owner of the drone rather than take the blame and possible financial repercussions of replacing the device.

Molly slowed to a stop and listened. The sound of an engine was heading in her direction.

Her pulse rocketing, she raced back up the trail, pulled her ATV out of the bushes and started the engine. Then she spun the vehicle around. But not fast enough.

She looked back in time to see another four-wheeler careen around the bend in the trail, the rider dressed all in black, wearing a black helmet, barreling straight for her.

Fear pinched her gut as she thumbed the throttle, sending the four-wheeler shooting forward and upward along the rocky trail, bouncing like popcorn in a kettle. She held on to the handgrips as her bottom left the seat again and again.

The ATV behind her slowly closed the distance.

At another bend in the trail, Molly risked a glance back. The rider had stopped in the middle of the trail, pulled a handgun and was pointing it at her.

She had two choices, continue on her way up the trail, in full view and range of the man's gun, or throw herself off the vehicle and down the side of the trail, tumble down a steep hill and risk breaking every bone in her body, but possibly living to see another day.

Molly released the handles, kicked off and away from the vehicle, and lunged toward the edge of the trail. She flew through the air for what felt like a very long time before she hit the side of the steep hill and tumbled, cartwheeled and slid down the rocky hill to the bottom where a huge boulder broke her downward trajectory.

With only moments to spare, she hauled her aching body up to her hands and knees and crawled behind the boulder where she collapsed, the light dimming around the edges of her vision and finally blinking out.

CHAPTER 4

KUJO HAD ONLY BEEN in Montana for two days. After Bear and Duke's visit to him in Colorado, he'd driven to San Antonio, where he'd spent a week filling out paperwork and convincing the trainers at Lackland he was fit to adopt Six, and that the dog and he were still a good match.

When he'd arrived at the kennels where the dogs were kept, he'd been hard pressed to keep his shit together. Since leaving the Army, he'd had nothing to do with dogs or the people who trained them. Nor had he been around men in uniform.

The range of feelings washing over him had kept him glued to the seat of his truck. He'd taken several minutes sitting in his pickup, gathering the courage he needed to face the very things he'd worked so hard to forget—the career he'd trained for, the dogs he'd loved and the only life he'd ever known.

When the sergeant in charge led him back to Six's kennel, no amount of mental coaching prepared him for the rush of emotion that nearly brought him to his knees.

As they approached, Six sat at the back of the kennel, his tail curled beneath him, his shoulders slumped and the light completely drained from his eyes.

"He's been like this since the people at his last foster home returned him," the sergeant said. "Nobody can reach him. He's non-responsive and completely shut down." The man pointed to the full bowl at the corner of the cage. "He hasn't eaten anything in three days."

Kujo had to swallow hard several times before he could voice a command. When he finally could squeeze air past his vocal cords, all he could manage was, "Six, come."

The dog's ears twitched, and his nose lifted slightly as if sniffing the air.

Kujo waited, afraid to say anything for fear of revealing just how devastated he was by the appearance of the dog that had saved his life.

For a long moment, the dog sat, sniffing the air. Then he rose up onto all fours, his tail drooping, and took a step forward.

Kujo opened the gate, stepped inside and pulled out of his pocket the old tennis ball he'd kept with his gear all those years. He squatted on his haunches and repeated, "Six, come."

Six sniffed the air, his ears now standing straight, his body tense. One step at a time, he eased toward Kujo, limping slightly.

"He took a hit from shrapnel on his last deployment," the sergeant offered.

Kujo barely heard the man. His attention remained on the dog, his gaze meeting Six's, silently urging him to close the distance between them.

When at last he did, Six sniffed at the ball, took it from Kujo's hand, and then he collapsed against him, whining, wiggling and cuddling until the weight of his body pushed Kujo over, forcing him to sit on the concrete.

Since then, Six had stuck to him like flypaper, refusing to leave his side.

From San Antonio, he'd driven all through the night, stopping only to put gas in his truck and to let Six out to stretch and do his business. Normally, he would have kept Six in a crate, like he had when he'd been in training or transporting him. But he figured they were both retired. To hell with the crate.

Six lay on the seat behind Kujo and occasionally stuck his nose over Kujo's shoulder and licked his face.

The dog had picked up bad habits over the years he'd been away from Kujo, but it didn't matter. All that mattered was that he and Six were a team once again.

When he arrived in Eagle Rock, Montana in the foothills of the Crazy Mountains, Kujo had driven straight up to Hank Patterson's house, introduced himself and asked if the job offer was still good.

Hank had welcomed him, given him a bed to sleep in for the night and briefed him the next morning about the work they were doing and his expectations of the people he hired to provide protective services.

At the moment, Hank was negotiating with a client who was coming to Montana in a few weeks and would need someone to work as a bodyguard. As all of his men were currently assigned, that job would be the one he'd assign Kujo. In the meantime, he could either stay with Hank, his wife and baby, or find a place of his own.

Kujo had gone out the next day and found a cabin in the mountains to rent. It wasn't much more than one room with a bed, small kitchen area and an outhouse. He suspected it was someone's old hunting cabin. The isolation suited him. The only drawback was the lack of telephone or cell phone reception. He figured he could rent the place for a few weeks while he waited for his assignment. It would give him time to acclimate to the town of Eagle Rock and the people in the community. Once a day, he'd visit town and check in with Hank.

The solitude would give him time to work with Six.

After moving into his cabin, Kujo had gone hiking in the mountains to work out the kinks of his long road trip, when Six had finally run ahead of him instead of clinging to his legs, refusing to leave his side.

The dog had separation anxiety from having been passed from one handler to the next, and then one foster home to the next. As far as Kujo was concerned, Six was now settled with his last owner. And Six seemed to know it. He'd finally left Kujo's side and raced ahead on the mountain trail, circling back to make sure he was still there and then running ahead again.

When the dog hadn't returned after a period of time Kujo was comfortable with, he'd picked up his pace, until he was jogging, trying to catch up to Six.

When he'd emerged from the tree line to find Six

41

with a woman squatting next to him, he'd been both relieved and a little angry. And he'd taken his anger out on the woman.

He didn't want to admit to himself she'd awakened in him something he hadn't felt in a long time. Attraction. When she'd given him just as much trouble as he'd given her, he couldn't help but admire her gumption.

At first, he couldn't understand why a lone woman would be out in the wilds of the mountains alone. But then he'd noticed she was probably packing a pistol beneath the leather jacket she wore. The telltale bulge around her waist had nothing to do with the gentle swell of her breasts above.

Her green eyes had sparkled when she'd been angry with him for being less than forthcoming with his reasons for being so high up on the trails, wandering the mountain, just him and his dog.

If he was still the same man he'd been before the explosion that got him medically boarded out of the Army, he might have teased her, or cajoled her into giving him her number.

But what good would that have done? He'd been out of the dating scene for three years. What woman wanted a washed-up Delta Force soldier with a limp? What did he have to offer to a relationship when all he'd done for the past three years was to bury himself in the woods, refusing to take part in life? All he had to show for all that lost time was a fixed-up cabin he couldn't even call his own.

His friends had been right. He owed it to himself and Six to get on with his life. Patterson had given him the opportunity he needed to make a new start, hopefully doing work he was still cut out for.

Dating and women would have to wait on the back-burner until he had something to offer in a relationship.

As he'd continued along the path through the woods, down into a valley and up to the top of the next ridge, he'd pushed himself physically. During his years in the Colorado Rockies, he'd climbed rocky hillsides, increasing his lung capacity and the muscles in his bum leg.

Deep in his heart, he'd harbored a dream of regaining enough of his old physical abilities to convince the medical board to reinstate him in the military.

He snorted and paused at the top of the ridge.

Like the Army would ever want a broken-down soldier among able-bodied men. He and Six had outlived their usefulness for the Army, their injuries sidelining them from doing the jobs they were trained to do. The sooner they both accepted their new normal, the sooner they could get on with the business of establishing new lives for themselves.

As he stood looking out over a valley, a movement caught his attention. Below him, something flashed and moved in a straight line along the valley floor.

He squinted, trying to make out what he was looking at. Finally, he realized the flying object was a drone, hovering in front of several caves in the side of a rocky escarpment.

At the moment he identified the drone, a shot rang

out. The drone tilted sideways and then dropped out of the sky, crashing into a stand of trees.

An engine roared to life at the top of the ridge opposite from where he stood. A dark smudge moved across the terrain and away from the valley. It appeared to be an ATV much like the one the woman called Molly had been standing so close to when Kujo had confronted her about petting Six.

Another engine fired up from a different location, deeper in the valley.

Kujo assessed the scene. One vehicle turned around on the mountain trail, a second ATV raced upward to meet the other. He assumed they were working together, until he saw the rider of the lower vehicle stop and raise both arms as if aiming at the person on the other ATV.

All of the sudden, the rider on the upper ATV flew through the air and over the edge of what appeared to be a cliff.

Kujo tensed and started running across the ridgeline toward the scene of the accident. The second vehicle came to a halt, the rider leaped off and stood at the side of the trail, looking down and holding something in his hand.

What was he doing?

Kujo wished he had a pair of binoculars. He narrowed his eyes, focusing on the man standing at the edge of the cliff. As he moved closer, he could make out the shape of the object in the man's hand.

It was a handgun.

Now running all out and doing his best to ignore

pain flaring in his bum leg, Kujo knew he had to get to the driver who'd gone over the edge before the man with the weapon fired.

The sharp report of gunfire echoed off the hillsides. Five rounds were discharged before the man with the gun climbed onto his ATV and headed over the top of the hill, disappearing out of sight.

Kujo ran as fast as he could, Six by his side, but the rough terrain slowed his progress as he slipped and slid in the rocks and loose gravel. When he got to the point on the trail where the abandoned ATV had come to a halt against a tree trunk, he stopped, sucked in deep breaths, and stared over the edge.

When he peered downward, he couldn't see signs of anyone below. At the bottom of the steep slope were several giant boulders.

Six sniffed the ATV, the ground, and then lifted his head. Before Kujo could stop him, he leaped over the edge and half-slid, half-loped down the slippery, steep hillside to where it bottomed out in front of the boulders. Then he ducked out of sight, behind the huge rocks.

Kujo waited for the dog to reappear. When he didn't, Kujo had no choice but to follow.

He stepped over the edge and started slowly down the hill. But the ground was nothing but loose rocks and gravel. Once he started sliding, there was no stopping until he reached the bottom. At first, he skied, balancing on both feet. Eventually, he sat, using his bottom as a sled, taking him all the way to boulders.

Fortunately, other than a sore tailbone, he arrived

relatively unscathed and leaped to his feet to follow the direction Six had gone. Behind the boulders, he found a dark lump lying against the ground. Six stood over the mass, licking something.

As Kujo moved closer, dread knifed through him as he realized the lump of black was the woman who'd introduced herself as Molly, and Six was licking her face. *Jesus, don't let her be dead.*

"Six, sit," Kujo commanded.

Six gave the woman one last kiss and sat back on his haunches, his eager brown eyes shifting from Molly to Kujo. He let out a worried whine, and then waited for Kujo's next command.

Molly laid still, not a muscle moved and her eyes were closed.

Kujo squatted next to her and felt for a pulse at the base of her throat. His gut clenched when he didn't feel the reassuring thump of a heartbeat against his fingertips. He shifted his hand and let go a sigh of relief when he located the strong, steady rhythm. She was alive but had suffered quite a fall.

Although afraid to move her, he knew he couldn't leave her where she was long enough to get off the mountain and call for help. Her attacker could return, or some scavenging animal might find her.

He shot a glance at Six. He could leave the dog and return with help, but he hadn't been with Six long enough to know whether he'd stay until Kujo returned.

No, he couldn't leave the woman. He touched her shoulder gently. "Molly."

She didn't respond.

He spoke louder. "Molly, wake up."

She stirred and moaned.

"Molly, you have to tell me what hurts."

For a long moment she didn't respond, but then she whispered, "Everything."

He chuckled. "Could you be more specific?"

"No," she said.

He had to lean close to hear her response.

"Can you move your fingers and toes?" he asked. Kujo stared at her hand, lying on the rocks beside her face. The digits moved slightly. He glanced at her feet, but boots covered her toes. If she moved them, he couldn't tell. "How did that feel?"

"Not bad," she said. Still her eyes remained closed.

"Did you feel your toes?"

She started to nod, but winced and then stilled, emitting a pathetic whimper. "Head hurts."

"Tell me if anything I touch causes you pain." Kujo wrapped his hands around her arms and squeezed gently, moving from the shoulder down to her wrists. "Anything hurt?"

"No."

"Could you feel my hands?"

"Yes."

"Good." He repeated the technique on the other side with the same reaction. Then he moved to her legs. Starting at her thighs he swept his hands down one leg. "Can you feel my hands?"

"Mmm."

His lips quirked. "Is that a yes?"

"Yes. Feels good," she said, and her eyes opened,

rounded and then closed again. "Did I say that out loud?"

He let go of some of his tension in muted laughter. "Yes, but you probably won't remember tomorrow, so don't worry about it."

"But you'll remember," she said, laying her arm across her eyes. "And you don't like me."

"I didn't say that."

"I could tell," she said, her voice fading.

"Molly, do you think you can sit up?"

"Sure," she said. As if to prove her words, she pushed herself to a sitting position with a little help from his arm supporting her.

"How's the back? Any pain?"

"I feel like I was run through a rock tumbler." She swayed and would have fallen over if he hadn't placed his hand behind her and held her upright. "I'm all right," she said. "I just need a little help standing."

"Are you sure you can?"

She nodded and winced again, then pressed a hand to the back of her head. "I can do this."

"If you're sure."

"Please, just help me stand so that I can assess the damage." She gripped the front of his shirt.

He wrapped an arm around her back. "On three. One...two...three." He stood, more or less pulling her up with him.

When she was upright, her fingers curled into his shirt, and she smiled. "See? I'm fine." Then she passed out, going completely limp in his arms.

Molly almost slid back to the earth. If Kujo had not

held on, she would have ended up back on the ground, possibly injuring herself even worse.

Six whimpered and leaned against Kujo's leg.

"You don't know the half of it, buddy. At least you don't have to carry her back up the hill."

He scooped her legs up and cradled her against his chest then emerged from behind the rocks. A quick evaluation of the slippery hillside had him formulating another plan. If he walked along the base of the hill, he'd come to a less vertical slope. Then he might stand a better chance of climbing while carrying an inert woman.

He started out, keeping a cautious watch out for the man who'd chased her down and shot at her after she'd fallen down the hill. If he showed up again, Kujo needed to be ready.

Something between him and her dug into his ribs, he glanced down and noticed the shoulder holster beneath her jacket and the 9-millimeter pistol.

He smiled. As he'd suspected, she'd come to the mountains packing. If the shooter returned, he could defend them. He wondered why she hadn't stopped and set up a defensive position, instead of falling over a cliff. She must have been as surprised as he was by the attack. Only someone desperate to avoid being shot would have chosen throwing herself off a cliff as a viable alternative.

His leg ached with the additional weight, but he trudged onward, slowly climbing through the trees and boulders. At a point when the slope grew steeper, he stopped and laid her over his shoulder, freeing one of his arms to better balance himself as he climbed. By the time he reached the old mining road, he was breathing hard, and his legs felt like they were on fire. Before he stepped out of the shadows, he checked both directions, held his breath and listened for the sound of an ATV engine.

He heard nothing but the wind stirring the lodge pole pines. Kujo and Six backtracked along the trail. Having walked more than five miles into the mountains, he knew he couldn't carry the woman all the way back. He had to get her out on the four-wheeler she'd ridden.

The ATV was wedged against the trunk of a tree. Though the handlebar was bent, the vehicle appeared to be intact.

He laid Molly on the ground, dragged the ATV away from the tree and hit the starter switch. The engine turned over and died. Kujo hit it again, and the motor roared to life. Shifting into neutral, he set the brake and returned to Molly's prone body.

Six stood guard beside her, refusing to move until Kujo lifted her into his arms and carried her to the ATV. How he was going to drive the ATV and hold onto the woman was an entirely different challenge. He straddled the seat and draped her body over his arm, resting her bottom across his thighs. It wasn't the most efficient way to get a person out of the mountains, but it would have to do.

Now, where to take her?

She had to have come up from one of the roads leading to the highway.

Unfamiliar with the trails, his best bet would be to take her back to his cabin, load her into his truck and drive her into Eagle Rock and the nearest medical facility.

Balancing Molly against his chest, Kujo shifted the ATV into gear and set off at a sedate pace back the way from which he'd come.

The five miles back to the cabin took over an hour. Six trotted alongside with his uneven gait. By the time he reached the cabin, Kujo's arms ached with the effort of maneuvering the four-wheeler and keeping Molly from slipping off his lap.

Six climbed the porch and flopped down, tongue lolling. He didn't move as Kujo dismounted the ATV and carried Molly toward the truck.

When he arrived there, he stood her against the truck, his body pressed to hers to hold her in place, and fumbled with the handle.

"Where are we?" she asked, blinking her eyes open.

"At my cabin about to get into a truck to take you to the hospital." He opened the door and would have laid her on the front passenger seat, but her hand shot out to grip the truck's door, blocking him from sliding her into the truck.

"No."

Tired, achy and past cranky, Kujo frowned down at the woman in his arms. "You need to see a doctor. You could have a concussion, maybe even swelling on your brain. And Lord knows if you've suffered any spinal cord injuries."

"Don't take me to town."

"Why?"

Her head lolled against his chest, and she closed her eyes again.

"Molly, I need an answer."

"Please, don't take me to town."

"Where else would I take you?"

"I don't know. But if the man who shot at me finds out I didn't die, he might not be happy about it."

"All the more reason to get you to a hospital, and then call the sheriff to report what happened."

She gripped his shirt. "Please, don't."

"I don't understand. A man shot at you. Do you want to ignore that fact? What if he targets another person?"

"I can't let him know he wasn't successful. It's better if he thinks I'm dead."

"I'm taking you to the doctor. You're delirious and not making any sense." He started to slide toward the open door again, but her hand on the doorframe put a crimp in his effort. "Woman, you've been a thorn in my side since we met."

"You're not a bundle of happiness, yourself," she whispered with her eyes still closed. Then she opened them and stared up into his gaze.

Those green orbs pierced him to the heart.

"Please."

Well, damn. When she put it that way, with the plea in her eyes as well as in her voice, how could he say no?

He sighed. "Where do you want me to take you?"

"Can't go back to my room in Eagle Rock," she mumbled. Then she shot a glance toward the old hunting cabin and the surrounding wilderness. "This place looks deserted. How about here?"

Kujo shook his head. "No way."

"Why?" she asked.

"Because it's *my* place, and I don't share it with women."

"For a couple days?" she pleaded, her voice fading as her body seemed to lose all the muscles holding it together. "I promise not to be a pain—"

"Sweetheart, it's too late for that kind of promise. You've been nothing but a giant pain in my ass since I ran into you on the ridge earlier."

Since she'd already passed out again, he had no choice. Lifting her in his arms, he marched across the clearing to the porch steps and climbed up to where Six lay, taking it all in as if he'd known all along the woman wasn't going anywhere.

"Traitor," Kujo said as he kicked the door to the cabin open and carried Molly inside.

Six slipped inside before the door swung shut.

CHAPTER 5

MOLLY FADED in and out of consciousness. One moment she was being held in the arms of her rescuer, bouncing along a mountain trail. Dust kicked up around her, but she didn't have the will to cough. She knew she should sit up and get herself off the mountain, but she didn't have the energy. So, she rested her cheek against the solid wall of Joe's chest and gave herself permission to go back to a very disturbed sleep where she couldn't quite rest because her bruised body was being jolted until her teeth rattled in her head.

When the vehicle finally came to a halt, her head cleared long enough for her to think. Whoever had been shooting at her probably assumed she was dead. Which might be a better position to be in to continue her investigation. She'd have at least a few days to recuperate and lay low, giving the B&B time to report her missing. The missing person report would support her cover of being dead. The person who'd shot at her wouldn't be concerned she'd mouth off to the authorities, and she'd have time to find the camp before the terrorists scrambled to leave the area.

Convincing "Just Joe" that she didn't need to go to the hospital had been exhausting. Once he'd agreed, she'd faded out again.

How long she'd been out, she didn't know. When she opened her eyes again, she had to blink several times. The room was so dark she'd thought she might have dreamed opening her eyes.

A dim light shined in the far corner of the dark room. As her vision cleared, she noted a potbellied stove glowing orange through a cast-iron grate.

She turned her cheek against the coarse fabric of a wool blanket and a damp nose bumped into her skin.

Molly jerked back and grinned when Six placed a paw on her arm and again nudged her with his snout.

"Hey, boy," she said, her voice hoarse. When she tried to move her arms and legs, a shadow crossed the room and hovered over her.

Joe sat on the edge of the bed, slipped a hand beneath her shoulders and helped her rise up just a little.

Again, she groaned. "If this is being alive, death might have been preferable."

"Take this." He held out a capsule.

She frowned. "What is it?"

"A painkiller."

Her frown deepened. "How do I know it's not some date rape drug?"

"Lady, if I'd wanted to rape you, I could have done it any time in the past twenty-four hours."

"Twenty-four hours!" She sat up straight and immediately regretted the sudden movement. Her strained muscles and bruises joined forces across her body to hurt all at the same time.

She collapsed against his arm, biting hard on her bottom lip to keep from crying out.

He shook his head. "Ready to take the pill?" Joe held it to her lips.

Obediently, she opened her mouth and took the offering, her lips touching his rough hands in the process.

He reached behind him for the tin cup on the nightstand beside the bed and held it to her lips. "Drink. You're probably dehydrated after being out for so long. I was going to take you into town if you didn't wake up soon."

Molly swallowed the pill and drank several more sips before leaning back. "I'm sorry to be so much trouble."

"I don't understand why you don't want to see a doctor. The kinds of injuries you sustained could kill you or leave you paralyzed for life."

"I can move." She raised her arm and winced at the number of bruises marring her skin. Then she noticed she wasn't wearing the shirt she'd had on when she'd fallen down the hill. Frowning, she shot a glance at Joe. "This isn't my shirt." Heat blossomed in her cheeks when she moved her legs against the coarse wool blanket. The prickly fabric abraded her skin. She grabbed the edge of the blanket and pulled it up to her chin. "Where are my clothes?"

Joe's lips twitched. He turned toward the potbellied stove and pointed at a line strung from one wall to another in the cozy room. On it hung her jeans, shirt, jacket and shoulder holster.

"My pistol?" she demanded.

"It's on the table by the stove. You can have it when you can hold it up."

"Did you...undress me?" she asked, her voice dropping to a whisper.

He straightened, set the cup on the nightstand and went to the stove. "Since you refused to go to a doctor, I had to make sure you didn't have any other injuries that needed attending. Removing the clothing allowed me to check you all over. After I cleaned your wounds, I couldn't put dirty clothing back on you." He nodded toward her drying shirt and pants. "I washed them. They should be dry by now."

So, the big T-shirt that enveloped most of her body was one of his. She should have known. It smelled like him. A hint of musk and the woodsy scent of the outdoors. Despite the aches and pains from sliding halfway down a mountain, her body responded to the man, her core tightening. Her lips still tingled where they'd touched his hand.

Heat burned her cheeks at the thought of those big, rough hands touching her skin, brushing across her thighs as he'd pulled off her jeans. After a little wiggle, she could tell she still had on her panties and bra. God, had he removed them and put them back on her? She felt completely exposed and at his mercy. "You shouldn't have removed my clothes without my permission."

"You didn't give me much of a choice. I would gladly have handed you over to the doctors and nurses at the emergency room and let them tally the wounds."

She bit down on her lip. Yeah, she should be grateful he'd carried her down from the mountain and taken care of her. He didn't have to. She wasn't his responsibility. She wanted to be mad at him, but she couldn't, since he'd gone to all the trouble to make certain she'd lived. "I suppose I should thank you," she said, reluctantly.

He nodded. "As it is, I'm not equipped with enough bandages and supplies for someone with as many cuts and scrapes as you have. I need to make a run to town. I could drop you off anywhere you would like. Even the hospital, if you've changed your mind."

Even before he finished the sentence, she shook her head. "I'd rather not go back until I figure out what exactly happened."

"I can tell you what happened. I saw it all from the opposite end of the ridge." His brows dipped into a fierce frown. "You jumped off your four-wheeler and fell to the bottom of a very steep hill. Then the guy on the other ATV shot at you. I take it you don't know who he was?"

Molly nodded. "I have no idea who would want to shoot at me."

"And then there's the matter of the drone he shot down first."

Molly's eyes widened as the reason she'd been out

there in the first place finally came back to her. "Oh, dear Lord." She flung back the scratchy blanket and started to swing her legs over the side of the bed. The pain of movement, made her cry out. Then she glanced at her legs, appalled at the huge cuts and bruises making her skin look like the canvass of an angry painter.

Joe stood in front of her, blocking her from getting out of the bed.

Not that she could. Her muscles screamed and some of the bruises and cuts throbbed.

"Where do you think you're going?'

"I need to find my drone and the controls." God, her boss was going to kill her. She had to get to the device and see if there was anything to salvage.

"The drone crashed in the trees. More than likely it's nothing more than scrap metal or plastic now."

"Yeah, but I need to collect all of the pieces. There was a camera on it too."

"It'll have to stay where it went down until you're well enough to climb around in the mountains."

When she tried to rise again, he laid a hand on her shoulder and applied the slightest pressure. "Stay."

Molly glared. "I'm not your dog to be trained and fed treats." As soon as the words left her mouth, her stomach grumbled as if to prove her wrong. She'd gone more than twenty-four hours without food. Her belly was reminding her of the fact. She also realized it wasn't fair for this man to have to feed, clothe and care for a stranger. "I should leave. You've done more than enough to help me."

"Where will you go?"

"Back to the bed and breakfast in town."

"And as soon as you do, the shooter will know you're still alive. Not that I have a stake in this situation, but you seemed to care a lot about hiding the fact you're still alive, thus the reason for your insistence on staying here." He walked to where her clothes hung on the line near the fireplace and lifted a gadget from the table. "I found this in the four-wheeler's basket. He held it out.

Molly stared at the device. "Oh, thank God." The controls had a built-in recording device. "I don't suppose you have a television or computer here?"

Joe snorted. "There's not one for at least a five-mile radius. We don't even have radio or cell phone reception out this far."

She chewed on the tip of her fingernail. "Electricity?" For the first time, she noticed the cabin didn't have a single light fixture—unless she counted the candles and oil lamp on the table.

"No."

"Holy hell, how do you live?"

Joe burst out laughing.

Six's ears perked, and he stared from Molly to Joe.

Up to that moment, Molly hadn't considered Joe that handsome. He'd been too serious and stone-faced to be considered traditionally handsome. However, he was ruggedly attractive, and when he smiled and laughed, he was stunningly gorgeous. The dark hair falling over his forehead and the twinkle in his brown eyes made her heart flip in her chest and her nipples tingle.

Damn, she should have better sense than drool over a man she'd just met.

He's seen me nearly naked.

Which didn't count since she'd been unconscious at the time. Still, this man knew more about her body than any other stranger off the street.

Joe held up his hand. "Look, stay here one more day, and I'll take you anywhere you want to go."

Molly frowned, trying to think of reasons she couldn't, but the bottom line was that she could only go back into town and, once she did, her attacker would know he hadn't killed her. Then it might become a race to see who could get to the downed drone first.

It had to be her. Until she was ready to go back into the woods, she'd be smarter to remain off-grid. That would give her time to recover from her injuries before she headed back out to that valley to retrieve the drone.

"Fine. I'll stay one more night. As long as you promise not to take advantage of me in the meantime."

He held up two fingers, Boy Scouts style. "I promise not to molest you, unless you want me to." With a wink, he lowered his fingers. He turned to Six. "Stay."

Six faced Joe, his tail sweeping the floor in rapid swipes.

Then Joe was gone, leaving Molly and Six alone in the dark cabin with only the light from the potbellied stove. The view through the door indicated it was light outside, though it was murky and dreary as if clouds covered the sun.

For a long time, Molly stared at the door through which Joe had disappeared. She knew nothing about him, but somehow she felt in her heart she could trust him.

Her glance went to the gun lying on the table. And apparently, he trusted her, especially since he'd convinced her to stay another day, instead of throwing her out on her injured ass. She could always get up, grab the gun and be out of there before he returned. She moved again and was reminded how badly movement hurt. The pill he'd given her was just beginning to take effect.

Molly yawned and lay back on the thin mattress.

Six laid his paw on her hand.

A chill settled over Molly, and despite the blanket wrapped snugly around her, she couldn't get warm enough. Once the shivers started, she couldn't stop them, and every tremble caused more pain, disturbing her stiff muscles and battered body.

The dog sniffed at her trembling body and whined quietly.

Molly patted the mattress beside her and said, "Up."

Six glanced toward the door and back to her. Then he crawled up on the mattress beside her, sharing his warmth.

She needed rest to allow her body to recover. Molly fell asleep, cuddling up to the German Shepherd. When she woke, she'd get that gun and be on her way.

CHAPTER 6

Kujo drove his truck into town and headed straight for the little pharmacy on the corner beside the grocery store. Not only was he out of bandages and disinfectant, he needed food for supper.

Molly would probably be better off with soup or something easy to eat or drink, but after his workout, Kujo needed a heartier meal.

For the past three years, he'd spent his life as a hermit, barely going to town for much more than the bare necessities. He still wasn't sure he was the right man for Hank's job. Guarding people would mean he'd have to actually interact with more and more *people*. Thankfully, his assignment wouldn't start for a little bit longer, which would give him time to acclimate himself back into society with all the noise and drama that accompanied so many people.

Kujo collected the medical supplies from the pharmacy then entered the grocery store to purchase enough food for the night. The cabin didn't have electricity, thus no way to refrigerate food. He'd have to shop on a daily basis. Yes, his choice of accommodations had given him a little transition time. He'd get his peace and quiet while at the cabin. At the same time, he'd be required to be more social when he came into town every day to get enough food for the day.

Inside the grocery store, he headed straight for the butcher counter where he selected a couple of thick steaks. Then he gathered potatoes and some broccoli. He topped off his basket with canned chicken soup, aluminum foil, salt and pepper.

The woman at the checkout stand smiled. "You must be new in town. I'd remember a handsome man like you." She held out her hand. "Mrs. Prichard. My husband and I own the grocery."

He took her hand and shook it, feeling uncomfortable with the attention when all he wanted was to pay for his purchases and get the hell out of this little burg. "Joe. Nice to meet you...ma'am."

"Joe? Do you have a last name, Joe?"

"Kuntz." Joe placed his items on the counter, hoping the woman would get on with adding up his total.

The older woman tipped her head and touched a finger to her chin. "I used to know some Kuntzs who lived up near Cut Bank. Are you related?"

Kujo shook his head. "My family is from Texas."

She brightened. "Oh, well. You never know." Mrs. Prichard rang up the items, bagged them and waited for Kujo to count out the money from his wallet. "Are you staying long?"

"Don't know," he answered noncommittally.

"Working yet?"

He shook his head.

Mrs. Prichard smiled. "I hear they could use more people at the Blue Moose Tavern. If you have ranching skills, there are plenty of people in these parts who need ranch hands. All you have to do is ask around."

"Thanks." Kujo held out his hand for the change, gathered his bags and left the store. He almost bumped into a big burly guy dragging a skinny woman with lanky hair by the arm, outside the door.

"Damn, woman, I told you I didn't want to be in town long. Move." He shoved her toward the grocery store hard enough she fell to her knees, and her purse flew across the sidewalk, spewing its contents.

"Goddamn it, now look what you've done." He grabbed her by her arm and jerked her to her feet. When she tried to bend back down to gather her purse and belongings, he shook her. "Leave it. It's just a bunch of junk anyway."

"Ray, that's my purse. It was a gift from my mother."

"Your old lady's dead. She won't know if you tossed it in the trash." The woman pulled her arm free and dove for the purse and the items rolling across the sidewalk.

The big burly man snarled and kicked the woman in the backside, sending her flying across the concrete.

Kujo carefully set his bags on the ground then grabbed Ray by the arm and spun him around. "Leave her alone."

"You know what? Maybe you should mind your own

business." The big guy cocked his arm and threw a hard punch straight for Kujo's jaw.

Kujo ducked to the side, caught the man's wrist, then twisted and pulled his arm up between his shoulder blades. "Maybe you should reconsider how you're treating that woman," he said, his voice low and threatening.

"Let me go, goddamnit!" Ray rolled his shoulders in an attempt to dislodge the man holding his arm.

Kujo kept his voice dead even. "I'll let go when you promise to be nice."

The woman laid a hand on Kujo's arm. "Sir, please don't."

Kujo shot a glance at the woman whose eyes were wide and round. "No man should treat a woman like he was treating you. Are you all right?"

"Martha's my bitch, so back off," Ray roared.

Kujo shoved the bastard's arm higher up his back. "Apologize to her for calling her names and abusing her."

"The hell I will," Ray grumbled.

"No, really, sir," Martha pleaded. "Let go of Ray. He doesn't mean to hurt me." Her voice shook. Apparently, she was terrified.

Kujo shook his head. "He shouldn't treat you that way. You don't have to put up with it."

"He's my husband."

"Yeah, but it doesn't give him the right to hit you. He's breaking the law."

"No, no, it's not like that. I wasn't hurrying fast

enough. I promise to be better next time, so he won't be angry."

"Seriously?" Kujo didn't understand the woman. "He has no right to hit you or throw you around like a rag doll. You can have him arrested on assault charges."

Ray snorted. "Tell him you love it," he said. "Tell him you beg me to treat you that way."

Martha shot a nervous glance toward Ray then nodded. "I do. I like it when he's...when he's mean to me."

Kujo's heart clenched when he noticed the yellowing bruise on her cheek. This woman had been abused on more than this occasion. She probably had been beaten enough to know to keep her mouth shut or she'd get it again when she reached home.

"Martha," he said, his voice softer. "I can go with you to the sheriff's department. You can file a complaint. They have shelters for women who are abused."

Ray bucked beneath Kujo's hold. "Don't be tellin' my woman she has to leave me. I married her fair and square. She's my property. She belongs to me."

"No one owns another person, asshole," Kujo said, pushing Ray's arm higher up his back.

The man stood on his toes, his face turning red from the effort to relieve the pain in his arm. "You might have me in a pinch now, but when you let go, I'm gonna kick your ass."

Kujo snorted. "Big words for a man who can't get out of a simple arm hold."

"Hey, what's going on here?" a deep voice called out from across the street.

Martha ran to the man crossing the street, wearing a law enforcement uniform. "Sheriff, you have to make him let go of Ray. You have to."

"Okay, okay, break it up." The sheriff stepped up to the two men, his hand resting on his service weapon, nestled in the holster at his hip. "Ray, have you been causing problems again?"

"I didn't do anything wrong when this man attacked me," Ray said.

The sheriff faced Kujo. "Sir, you'll have to let go of him."

Kujo didn't move. "After his wife tells you what Ray was doing to her when I stepped in."

Martha wrung her hands and shot glances from the sheriff to her husband "He wasn't doin' anything. I promise."

The sheriff looked from Martha back to Kujo. "Mister?"

"I stopped him from kicking and shoving his wife," Kujo said. "When I did, he took a swing at me. I merely defended myself."

Resting his hand on his service weapon, the sheriff said, "Well, I got you covered if you'd like to let go of him now."

Kujo gave the man a little shove before he released him, putting some distance between them in case Ray came out swinging.

Then he stepped back and turned to the sheriff while keeping an eye on Ray as the man rubbed his shoulder.

Martha slipped her hand through Ray's arm and clung to him.

"I'm Sheriff Barron." The sheriff held out his hand. "New in town?"

"I am." Kujo took the sheriff's hand in his. "Joe Kuntz. Just arrived."

"Wanna tell me what happened?"

"Yeah, right," Ray grumbled. "Get the story from the outsider. You should arrest him. He tried to break my arm."

"I'll hear both sides," Sheriff Barron said, focusing his attention on Kujo. "Start at the beginning, Mr. Kuntz."

Kujo told him what he'd observed and of the abuse Martha had suffered at her husband's hands.

"Martha?" The sheriff turned to Martha.

"I don't know what Mr. Kuntz is talking about. Ray's been a perfect gentleman." The woman ducked her head, refusing to look the sheriff in the eye.

"Sheriff," came a warbling voice from behind them. Mrs. Prichard stood in the doorway to her shop. "The newcomer had it right. I saw everything from my cash register. Ray was being an ass to poor Martha. This man had the balls to stand up to him."

Ray glared at Mrs. Prichard. "Stay out of it."

"Like hell I will." Mrs. Prichard planted her fists on her hips. "You've been badmouthing and picking on Martha since she agreed to marry your sorry ass. It's about time someone gave you what for."

"Is that right, Martha?" the sheriff asked.

Martha stood with her head down, tears trickling down her cheeks. "He doesn't mean anything by it."

"But he's hitting you and hurting you, isn't he?" the sheriff asked.

"Don't answer him, Martha," Ray warned. "You don't have to say anything. Don't let them put words in your mouth."

The sheriff glared at the big bully. "Ray Diener, you're under arrest for assault. You can come with me willingly, or we can do this the hard way."

"You can't arrest him," Martha cried. "I don't want to press charges. He didn't hurt me."

Mrs. Prichard slipped her arm around Martha's shoulders. "Honey, look at your knees and hands. They're all scraped from him shoving you to the ground and kicking you. He treats you worse than he treats his dogs."

"No, please, don't take him," Martha sobbed. "He's all I have. How will I live?"

"We'll get you settled," Mrs. Prichard said. "Don't you worry. That sorry excuse of a man won't hurt you ever again."

"Martha, if you go with them, we're over! You hear me?" Ray's brows dipped low on his forehead, and his gaze burned with hatred.

He swung a hand toward her, but Kujo stopped the meaty fist from making contact by blocking his arm with his.

Martha flinched and cowered.

Mrs. Prichard pushed Martha behind her. "Does it make you feel like more of a man to abuse someone half your size? The big bad man can hit a woman. Oooo, I'm so scared."

"You'll regret this," Ray warned, his gaze encompassing Mrs. Prichard, Martha and Kujo. "All of you. No one comes between me and what I own."

"You don't own Martha," the sheriff stated.

"She's wearing my ring, isn't she?" Ray demanded.

"That doesn't mean you own her. Everyone has a right to protection, even if it's protection from her own husband." The sheriff glared at Diener.

Mrs. Prichard hugged Martha. "Come on, sweetie. I know someone who can help you." She led Martha into the grocery store.

"Ray, hold out your hands," the sheriff said.

"This is bullshit," Ray yelled. "You're going to arrest me all because some outsider son-of-a bitch stuck his nose in where it doesn't belong?"

"No, Ray, I'm arresting you for assault. You can't beat Martha just because you're married."

"She's my wife!" The man lunged at Kujo.

Kujo had expected the man to do something stupid. He stepped aside.

Ray's momentum carried him past Kujo. He tripped on the curb and crashed to his knees, ripping his denim jeans. Stupid with anger, he staggered to his feet, spun and charged toward Kujo.

Sheriff Barron raised his hand and shot a stun gun at the big man. It hit him square in the chest, and he dropped like a bag of stones.

The sheriff shook his head, a smile curling his lips. "Always wanted to try that to see how it worked on someone besides my deputies." He nodded. "Glad to see it's effective." He switched the device off and slipped it into his pocket. Then he rolled Ray onto his stomach and cuffed his wrists behind his back.

"I'll need you to stop by the station and give your statement," the sheriff said.

Kujo nodded. "Will do."

A sheriff's deputy pulled up in a large SUV and jumped out. Together, Sheriff Barron and the deputy hauled Ray into the back seat and took him away, leaving Kujo standing in front of the grocery store, tense and ready to get back to his cabin in the wilderness. A hand touched his arm, and he spun in a low crouch, his fists clenched, ready to defend himself.

"Hey, slugger." Bear held up his hands. "It's just me."

Kujo dropped his hands and straightened. "Sorry, I just had a run-in with one of the locals."

"Oh, yeah? Anyone I know?"

"Ray Diener?"

Bear held up his hand at about Ray's height. "About this tall...dark and mean?"

"That about sums him up." Kujo gathered his grocery bags from the ground and walked to his truck.

Bear strode beside him. "I'm glad you decided to take Hank up on his offer. He said you showed up with a German Shepherd." Bear grinned. "I bet Six was happy to see you. How's he doing?"

"His injuries gave him a limp, but he compensates and gets around pretty well." Kujo shook his head, recalling how he'd gone running ahead of him and allowed Molly to pet him. "He needs refresher training, but I think he'll respond quickly."

Bear pounded him on the back. "Glad to hear it. I hated to think of that dog being put down because no one could handle him. He saved our butts enough times he deserves to live the rest of his life high on the hog."

"Yes, he does. But he still has some good years left in him. And he likes to work. No use retiring him just because he has a limp."

"Agreed." Bear glanced across the street. "I'm meeting some of the team at the Blue Moose. Care to join us?"

"I'll take a rain check. I have to get some things back to the cabin I'm renting and check on Six."

Bear glanced around. "That's right. He's not with you. I thought you'd took him everywhere you went."

"I do, for the most part." Kujo didn't want to lie to his friend, but he didn't feel like he could tell him about the woman in his cabin. Not yet. Molly said she wanted to keep her presence a secret from everyone. As long as no one saw him carry her into his cabin, no one knew she was there. He hoped she didn't plan on staying for days. Kujo had done his share of sleeping on the cold, hard ground. He didn't plan on doing it for long, if he could help it. Sleeping on the ground played havoc with his bad knee. "I'll join you another night."

"Hank said you're in an old hunter's cabin until you can find a place closer to town."

Kujo nodded.

"Is it true, no phone or electricity?"

Again, Kujo nodded.

Bear shook his head. "Better you than me. Mia wouldn't like it much if she couldn't blow-dry her hair in the morning."

Kujo eased his mouth into a smile. "That's right, you're married now. When do I get to meet Mia?"

"We're staying in the house her folks left to her here in town. But she's in Hollywood for the week, meeting with her agent about one of the scripts she wrote."

"Do you ever go with her?" Kujo asked.

"Depends on my assignments. I'm starting a new one in two days. I'll be providing protection to a Hollywood star while he's on vacation on his ranch in Montana."

Kujo shook his head. From the hills and dust of Afghanistan to the fancy ranches of the rich and famous in Montana, the Delta Force soldiers had come a long way. He arched an eyebrow. "It's a tough job."

Bear nodded. "But someone has to do it. And what better way to make a living outside the Army?"

Bear seemed to have come to terms with his role in the civilian world. Kujo hoped he'd find peace and a sense of purpose in his new job, too.

In the meantime, he had a hungry woman waiting for him in his cabin and a dog he needed to retrain practically from scratch. He had some bad habits, like licking pretty women.

Not that the idea hadn't slipped through his own consciousness. Molly had a beautiful body. One he'd had the pleasure of viewing as he'd stripped her out of her clothing to check her for any life-threatening wounds. "Bear, tell the others I'll meet up with them soon. I have to get back for now."

"I'll tell them. And for the record, you're welcome to stay in our house until you find a better location. You don't have to rough it out in the woods."

"Thanks. I'll keep that in mind."

Kujo loaded his groceries into the back seat of his pickup and climbed in.

Bear waved, crossed the street and entered the tavern.

In the past, back when Kujo had been part of the Delta Force team, he'd been eager to join his teammates for a drink after work.

Three years away had created distance between them. Kujo wasn't quite sure how to close that distance, or if he even wanted to. He hadn't realized how truly lonely he'd been until Bear and Duke had shown up on his doorstep. But fitting back into the social dynamics of a team might be something he could do slowly.

He drove past the tavern and the sheriff's office, where the sheriff and a couple of deputies struggled to move Ray from the back of the SUV and into the jailhouse.

Kujo didn't have time to worry about the bully who treated his wife like a doormat. He needed to get back and check on Six and Molly.

As he drove out of town and through the countryside to the road leading up to the hunting cabin, he wondered if the man who'd shot at Molly could have followed them back to the cabin. Kujo had been so focused on not dropping the unconscious woman, he couldn't be sure. He'd been moving slowly enough it wouldn't have been hard to trail them.

The more he thought about it, the more worried he became, until he was pushing his truck to go faster and faster. By the time he reached the narrow road leading up through the woods, he was flying over the bumps and ruts. He skidded to a stop in front of the cabin and hopped out of the truck.

When he unlocked and pushed open the cabin door, he nearly collapsed with relief.

A beam of light from the setting sun trailed across the floor to the bed where Six lay on the mattress.

Kujo didn't have the heart to be mad at the dog. Not when he moved closer to discover Molly on the other side of the big shepherd. Her eyelashes lay in dark crescents against her pale cheeks, and her full, luscious lips were parted as if in a sigh.

Six glanced up and started to move.

Kujo held up his hand in a motion to still the dog. "Stay," he said.

Six settled again, laying his head on his paws, his gaze following his master around to the other side of the bed.

Molly was pretty when she wasn't being a smartass. She had the face of an angel, but what had she been doing out in the mountains with a drone? And why would someone shoot down the drone, and then try to finish off the woman?

Perhaps the drone and the video footage captured by the camera would be the answer.

In the meantime, Kujo had a houseguest. A very pretty houseguest, who was full of sass. Hell, he didn't need these kinds of complications. With a new boss and a new job, he needed the opportunity to prove himself. Instead, he was stuck babysitting a woman who'd more or less invited herself into his cabin for who knew how long. And now, she was taking up his bed. He'd be damned if he slept on the floor for very long.

CHAPTER 7

THE DELICIOUS SCENT of grilled steak woke Molly's stomach before it actually woke her. A day and a half without food had that effect. Her belly rumbled loudly. Eventually, Molly opened her eyes and looked around the dark room for the source of the heavenly smell.

"Hungry?" a deep, rich voice asked from the other side of the small room.

The reassuring weight of the German Shepherd was gone, and the cool air made her shiver.

"Do I smell food?" she said, her voice cracking.

"Steak and potatoes. My cooking skills are limited."

"Sounds wonderful." She pushed up on her elbows, the movement waking up all the battered and bruised parts of her body. Still, the pain wasn't nearly as bad as the first time she'd made the same attempt. The pill she'd taken earlier must have given her some relief.

He loaded a plate and carried it over to her.

"I can eat at the table." Molly tried to get out of the bed, swinging her bare legs over the edge. The chilly, mountain air made her immediately regret her decision to get up. "You don't have to serve me," she muttered. Molly's independent streak, the one that got in the way of most of her relationships couldn't be ignored. Well, maybe just this once.

She glanced at the smooth planks on the floor and imagined they would be icy cold. Her bare toes curled at the thought of touching the wood.

Joe set the plate on the nightstand, scooped her legs up and tucked them back under the covers. "Stay in the bed until I have a chance to put something on your cuts and scrapes."

"I can do that myself. You don't have to do anything else for me." She wasn't used to having anyone wait on her.

"I haven't done much," he said.

But he had carried her out of the woods, up and over the mountain and cooked dinner for her. Molly inhaled deeply, drawing in the heavenly scent of charbroiled steak.

Joe reached for the plate, handed it to her and went back to get his. He grabbed a chair and stood it next to the bed and sat beside her.

Six curled up on the floor nearby.

Leaning against the wall, Molly rested the plate on the blanket in her lap, cut off a slice of the juicy steak and placed it in her mouth. The juices danced across her taste buds. As she chewed, she closed her eyes, leaned back her head and moaned. "Sweet Jesus, that was amazing."

A quick glance at her rescuer revealed his lack of

agreement and a positively frowning countenance. "Are you always this emotional about your food?"

She sighed. "Only when it's orgasmic. This is better than sex," she said before thinking and popped another bite of the steak in her mouth, hoping he'd let the comment pass.

He didn't. "Apparently, you haven't had good sex." Joe took a bite and chewed before speaking again. "What were you doing out in the mountains yesterday that would warrant someone shooting at you?"

And so started the interrogation... Molly didn't have the clearance to tell Joe about her operation. A twinge of guilt knotted her gut as she opened her mouth prepared to lie.

"Don't say anything if it means you have to lie."

She blinked. "You don't know I was going to lie."

"You hesitated, looked away and gathered a whopper of a story before you opened your mouth. It was going to be a lie." He shook his head. "I'm good at reading people."

She pressed her lips together and glared at him. "Oh, yeah? What am I thinking right now?"

He chuckled. "That you hate me for outing you before you could concoct your story. That you'd like to throw your plate at me, but you're too hungry to waste the food. And you're wondering if sex with me could possibly be as good as that steak." Joe shoved another bite of steak into his mouth and chewed.

Molly opened her mouth and closed it again. The man had been spot on. Damn him. "I wasn't thinking what sex would be like with you. And you're being all creepy, talking about it when you have me at your mercy."

He shrugged and polished off the steak on his plate. "Finish your meal. I'm going out to get more wood for the stove. Don't get dressed yet. I got ointment and bandages that need to be applied."

He stood, laid his plate in a tin pail and opened the door to the cabin, letting in a cool breeze.

Molly shivered.

Outside, darkness had wrapped its mystery around the man and the mountain, cutting them off from the rest of the world and making the setting even more intimate than in the daylight.

Six trotted out onto the porch.

Joe followed and closed the door behind them.

Inside the relative warmth of the cabin, tucked into the rough woolen blanket, Molly stared at the door, her pulse pounding against her ribs. The man was entirely too cocky. To think she would be interested in anything sexual with him was ridiculous.

So what if he had incredibly broad shoulders, arms that could lift her up as if she weighed no more than a child, and a smile that turned her knees to noodles. Molly had to remind herself he'd been rude and less than forthcoming with information about himself. Much like herself.

His name was Joe. Just Joe. First thing she had to do was get his full name and have her contacts back in DC run him against the National Crime Information Center database to see if they found a match. Of course, he could give her a fake name, which might result in a bogus hit. For all she knew, the man could be a serial killer.

"Doubt it," she said out loud. "He has a nice dog." Yeah, the conclusion wasn't scientific, but she liked Six, and Six liked both of them. Dogs, for the most part, were good judges of character.

But it wouldn't hurt to run him through NCIC, just to be safe.

He could have killed you by now, she reminded herself. Joe could have left her for dead out in the mountains. No one would have found her until the scavengers had picked her bones clean—if anyone found her at all.

Molly chewed on that and another piece of the amazing steak. The man had talent when it came to cooking beef.

Minutes later, Joe entered the cabin, carrying an armload of wood. He set the load beside the stove then grabbed the pail and left the cabin again.

Six stayed inside this time, taking up a position beside her bed.

"He doesn't talk much, does he?"

Six stared up at her with soulful brown eyes.

Molly glanced at the door, cut off a bite of steak and had it halfway to Six's mouth when the door opened, and Joe returned.

He frowned when he spotted her hand held out with the piece of steak. "Don't."

"It's just one piece."

"He's on a strict diet. Anything foreign might create problems in his digestive tract."

Six stared at the chunk of steak, and drool slipped out of the corner of his mouth.

"I'm sorry, boy," she whispered. She popped the steak into her mouth and chewed, her brows dipping as she glared at Joe. Once she'd choked down the offending morsel, she set the plate to the side. "One piece of steak?"

"One. I told you, he was a highly trained working dog." Joe set the pail on the stovetop and cleaned his plate and the skillet in which he'd cooked the steak. He collected her plate and made quick work of it as well.

After he stacked the plates on a shelf, he carried the pail back outside, tossed the water and returned with fresh, clean water. Joe wiped his hands, wet a washrag, and grabbed a towel and the bag, bearing the label of the local pharmacy, then sat in the chair beside the bed.

When he reached for the blanket covering her legs, he stopped short. "Do you mind? We need to treat some of those cuts and abrasions before they get infected."

Molly hesitated. The thought of Joe's big, coarse hands on her legs sent shivers all across her body and heat coiling at her core. Her tongue knotted in her mouth, so all she could do was nod.

Without preamble, he flung the blanket aside and stared down at the cuts, bruises and abrasions. Joe smoothed his hand over her thigh and down to her ankle, and then he went to work, cleaning the wounds and applying antibiotic ointment. When he'd completed the tops of her legs, he looked up. "Lie on your stomach. I'll take care of the backs of your calves and thighs."

"No, really. I can do that." She held out her hand for

the ointment, knowing perfectly well, she couldn't see all the damage and would botch the job. But having him stare at her backside for any length of time was just... just... Another shiver rippled through her body. The tops of her legs where he'd cleaned and treated her scrapes tingled everywhere his hands had been. How the hell was she supposed to play it cool and unaffected?

"Roll over," he commanded.

Six immediately complied.

Molly laughed, nervously.

Joe raised an eyebrow. "If Six can do it, you can, too. Come on. Some of these wounds had dirt ground into them. The sooner we get it out, the better."

Gathering the long T-shirt around her bottom, Molly rolled onto her stomach, her core tightening, and her sex aching.

This time, he started at the ankles and worked his way up the backs of her legs to her thighs. With the washcloth, he gently wiped the dirt out of the wounds. He smeared salve over the abrasions and applied bandages over the deeper cuts.

"Can't do anything about the bruises. When you get back to town, I recommend ice for the swelling.

The whole time Joe ran his hands across her legs, Molly couldn't stop the heat building inside. What would happen if he slid his hand between her legs and brushed against her center?

She swallowed hard on the moan rising up her throat. How could she have sexual fantasies about a man whose name she didn't know?

"What's—" Molly's voice squeaked. She cleared

her throat and tried again. "Joe, considering your know more about me than I ever thought possible, perhaps you could tell me your last name. Unless of course, it's a secret and you're in the witness protection program, in which case, you will likely tell me and then have to kill me." Holy shit. She was babbling. His touch was doing crazy things to her insides.

"Kuntz," he replied. "Do you always talk so much?"

"Only when I'm nervous."

"Nothing to be nervous about. I won't take advantage of the situation, if that's what you're concerned about."

Oh, hell, she wasn't worried about Joe taking advantage of her. She was worried he wouldn't. Or that he would, and she'd embarrass herself by begging for more.

He'd reached the tops of her thighs just short of the T-shirt hem. "I know you scraped your back in your fall. I need to get to it. Do you mind?"

"Hell, you've come this far and seen me practically naked when I was unconscious—what's the difference?" Except now, she was awake, and her body was reacting to his ministrations to the point she might orgasm before he finished.

"Exactly." He slipped her shirt up her back, his knuckles skimming across her skin, setting off an array of fireworks blasting along her nerve endings.

This is a very bad idea. Despite the fact he was treating stinging cuts, his touch felt so good, she couldn't say no, or stop, or anything any rational woman should say when nearly baring her all with a virtual stranger.

He wrung out the washcloth in the pail of water. "This is going to sting a little." Joe pressed the damp cloth to the scrapes on her back.

Molly hissed. More because of the brush of his knuckles against her skin than the stinging sensation created by rubbing the abraded skin.

"I cleaned these wounds last night, but I didn't have anything to put on them and no bandages."

"Thank you for taking care of me. I would have died had you not found me when you did," she said softly.

"Actually, I didn't find you. Six did," He said, leaning close enough, his warm breath stirred the hairs along the back of her neck.

She turned her head toward the dog and held out her hand.

Six nuzzled her fingers until she reached up and scratched behind his ears. "Aren't you going to tell me to stop touching your dog?"

"I'll work on his training later. He's still trying to readjust to me."

Molly frowned. 'Readjust?"

"He's been passed around from trainer to trainer and then to foster families. He needs time to settle, to feel like he's home to stay with one owner, one trainer." Joe continued to work on her back, cleaning and applying ointment.

"Sounds like he's had a rough time of it." Molly said.

Joe unclipped her bra.

Molly gasped and brought her hands up to the sides of her breasts. "What are you doing?"

"Dressing your wounds. I'll hook it back when I'm done."

"I certainly hope so."

A low chuckle rumbled close to her. "Relax."

"Easy for you to say," she grumbled. "You're not the one at the mercy of someone twice your size and strength."

His hand stilled. "Look. I don't know what kind of men you've been hanging out with, but I don't abuse women. Have I hurt you in any way?"

"No," she mumbled.

"And I won't. I don't need to hurt women to get off."

Molly's cheeks heated. The man had been more than a gentleman in his dealings with her, and she'd given him nothing but hell. "I'm sorry. I'm judging you without getting to know you." She cleared her throat. "Hi, I'm Molly Greenbriar." She couldn't turn her head far enough to look up at his expression.

"Joe Kuntz, but you already know that." He smeared ointment into the scrape across her back. "My friends call me Kujo."

Molly snorted. "I was okay with Joe and Kuntz, but Kujo isn't making me feel all warm and fuzzy."

"It worked when I was in the military."

"I can imagine. What were you, a Ranger or Special Forces?"

"Delta Force," he responded, his tone low, almost too hard to hear.

"I'm impressed." She stared at Six. "And Six?"

"He was my battle buddy. He and I led the way into enemy territory."

"Is he trained to attack?"

"No. He's a bomb-sniffing dog."

Molly reached out to touch Six's scar. "Is that how he got this?"

Joe applied a bandage over one of the deeper scrapes across her back. "That's what it says on his record."

"You weren't with him when it happened? I thought handlers stayed with their dogs?"

"That's usually the case, unless one or the other is injured."

Molly leaned up on her elbow, realized she was exposing her breasts, and covered them with her hands so that she could turn far enough to face Joe. "I'm confused. Obviously, Six was injured."

His face was a mask of stone, the only movement a muscle twitching in his jaw. "Six was injured three years after I was released from active duty."

Molly stared at the man, her eyes widening. "You were injured first?" She swept him from head to toe, lingering on his legs. "You were limping when I first met you. Was that what got you kicked out?"

Joe stared at her for a moment then dropped his gaze to the bandages on her back. "Yes."

"And you didn't get to take Six with you?"

"He wasn't injured as badly."

"But you were his handler." Molly couldn't imagine the two being apart. *How cruel.*

Joe shrugged. "He belonged to the Army. He still had good years left in him. A lot of time, money and effort went into his training." Again, Joe's jaw hardened. "He still had a job to do."

Joe didn't say the words *Even if I didn't*, but Molly heard them. The man had been injured and kicked out of the military, losing his friends, his dog and his job all at once.

"But you have Six now," Molly reminded him. She smiled. "And he seems happy to be with you. Are you going to train him to work in an airport or for the police department?"

"No." Joe hooked her bra together and pulled her shirt down over her back and bottom.

She tugged it over her thighs and pushed to a sitting position. "What kind of work are you doing now?"

"I've answered my quota of questions. It's your turn."

Molly closed her mouth on the next words she'd been about to say. She'd expected him to spill his guts, but she wasn't at liberty to reveal the real reason she was there.

"What is Molly Greenbriar doing in the mountains flying a drone?"

Feeling guilty over the fact she couldn't be honest with him, she lowered her eyes. "I'm filming footage of the mountains. I'm attempting to create my own documentary on the Crazy Mountains and the history surrounding them."

Joe's eyes narrowed. "Who are you working for?"

She'd practiced her answers to the point she could recite them without thinking. But something in Joe's countenance made her suddenly forget. "I...uh..." As her gaze met his, she couldn't look away and her mouth couldn't seem to form the words.

He cocked an eyebrow. "Is the question that hard?"

Heat rose up her neck and suffused her cheeks. "No. Of course, not. I'm...I'm freelancing. I was gathering information and footage I planned to look at later during the editing process. Which reminds me, I really need to recover the drone and see if it can be salvaged. It's key to my work here."

Joe didn't respond. Instead, he held her stare long enough to make her feel even more uncomfortable. He wasn't buying her story.

Molly fought to keep her face set and her body still. She refused to squirm under his scrutiny. This was her first assignment in the field. If she proved herself here, she might be considered for future field assignments. If she blew her cover in the first few days, she'd be back at a desk, performing background checks.

"I'm feeling a little better," she said, shifting her gaze from his.

"Liar," he countered.

Molly frowned. "I'm not lying."

"It's all in your body language." He reached out to brush his finger along her cheek. "Every time you say something untrue, you glance away."

"I do not!" She stared straight into his eyes, even as she fought the urge to look away.

"It's okay. I figure you have a reason for lying to me. Keep your secrets; I'm not interested. As long as they don't come back to bite me in the ass."

"Look, I can go back to my room in town. I don't want to inconvenience you."

"Too late for that." He chuckled. "You've been an inconvenience since I ran into you on that mountain trail."

Molly slid her legs over the edge of the bed. "Seriously, if you could give me a ride back to town, I'll be out of your hair. No. Never mind, I'll take the ATV."

He pressed a hand on her shoulder. "Don't get your panties in a wad. You're not up to riding a damaged ATV seven miles back to town in the dark. And as much as I'd like to have my cabin and bed back, I wouldn't feel comfortable leaving you alone in town. Not until we figure out who shot at you and left you lying out in the mountains for buzzards to pick through your bones."

"Now who's being overly dramatic?" Her lips curled upward. The man had rescued her. He deserved her gratitude. "Thank you for saving my life and treating my wounds."

"Don't thank me, thank Six." Joe tipped his head toward the dog.

Six had settled beside the bed with his chin on his paws. When he heard his name, he lifted his head, his ears perked.

Molly reached out to stroke his neck. "Thank you, Six. And despite being a bit cantankerous, your master isn't so bad himself." She faced Kujo again. "If you like, I can sleep on the floor. You shouldn't have to give up your bed for the second night in a row."

"Stay. You're still recovering. Besides it's cold on the floor. With your injuries, your body's immune system might be compromised." Again, he lifted her legs and tucked them beneath the blanket. "Get some rest. We'll figure everything out in the morning."

"Where will you sleep?" she asked.

He gave her a twisted grin. "In a chair or on the cold, hard floor."

Molly shook her head. "No way." She hesitated for only a moment before saying, "If you promise not to do anything, you can sleep in the bed. It's big enough for the two of us." Her cheeks heated at the thought of Joe slipping beneath the blanket, his long legs brushing against hers, his broad shoulders taking up most of the space. She'd been stretching the truth that time. The bed was big enough for Joe. Alone. "I sleep on my side, anyway."

She scooted to the far side of the mattress, turned her back to him and twisted around to nod at the space she'd created. "See? There's enough room if you sleep on your side."

Joe's brows dipped. "I'll be fine on the floor."

She shrugged. "Have it your way. But if you change your mind during the night, the offer's still open. I'll leave room for you." Molly settled on her side, resting her head on half of the pillow. She laid for a long time, feigning sleep, her ears straining to hear every sound coming from Joe.

He moved about the room, the floor creaking, marking his progress. She heard the clank of the cast-iron stove door opening and closing.

A cold breeze blew through the cabin as Joe opened the door, making Molly shiver. The click of toenails on the wooden floor indicated Six heading for the door for one last visit to the great outdoors before he settled in to sleep.

Molly dared to turn and look.

Joe stood for a moment in the door before following Six out onto the porch and closing the door behind him.

Molly didn't know much more about Joe than when she'd run into him on the mountain trail, but she knew she trusted him.

Her body ached, but she could handle it better. Sleep eventually claimed her, though she shivered in the cool cabin.

Sometime during the night, she dreamed of a dark stranger firing at her, of falling off a cliff, falling...falling...into a bottomless abyss. She cried out, afraid she would hit the ground and break into a million pieces.

Strong arms caught her and held her close. Half asleep, she snuggled up to the heat and slipped into a deep, deep sleep, finally feeling safe.

CHAPTER 8

KUJO HELD off as long as he could. He cleaned the dishes, stoked the fire and took Six out to do his business one last time before calling it a night.

No matter how long he stayed away from Molly, he returned, stared down at her sleeping form and spent time talking himself out of taking her up on her offer to share the bed.

But when Molly started thrashing, her arms and legs flailing in the air, he couldn't ignore her for a moment longer. Whatever dream she was having had to be bad, and it would be really crappy of him to ignore a woman in need, wouldn't it? And she might worsen her injuries, if she kept it up.

Kujo understood dreams. For the past three years, he'd woken in the middle of the night, sweating and reluctant to go back to sleep. His dreams consisted of the last few minutes before his life had changed and the lives of the two female soldiers had ended.

He could still imagine those women's faces, the

desperation in their eyes, and hear the explosion as it rocked his world forever.

Yeah, he understood dreams.

Six stood beside the bed, staring at Molly, his ears perking with every moan from the woman. He glanced back at Kujo and whined softly.

"It bothers you too, doesn't it?" Kujo crossed to Six and ran his hand over the dog's head and down his neck.

Six nuzzled his hand, and then used his nose to nudge Kujo toward Molly.

Kujo sat on the side of the bed and touched Molly's arm.

She moaned again and reached out to cover his hand with hers, her fingers gripping his like a lifeline.

Now what? He couldn't disengage and leave her hanging. Too late for second thoughts about touching her, he toed off his boots and slipped onto the mattress. As soon as he did, she rolled up against him.

The bed really was too small for two people. To keep from falling out, he turned on his side, facing her and spooned her body with his.

Molly sighed and turned toward him, resting her hand and her cheek against his chest. Her calf slid over his and hooked him from behind.

Kujo swallowed a groan. This was the reason he hadn't wanted to share the bed with her. Molly Greenbriar was entirely too pretty and sexy. A man had to be made of stone to ignore a body like hers pressed against him.

Kujo wasn't made of stone. Although his cock was

making a damned good imitation. He lay perfectly still, trying not to rub anything that would make him even harder and more uncomfortable. Being still didn't make a difference.

Molly's fingers curled into his shirt, her nails scraping his chest through the fabric. Her hair smelled of peaches, and her breath warmed his neck.

He gave up any pretense of sleep and stared at the woman in the fading light from the potbellied stove.

How had he gone from being a hermit in a Colorado mountain cabin to having a job and a woman in his bed, in such a short time?

His pulse pounded, and his staff stiffened. Perhaps that was the problem. He hadn't had a woman in over three years. His desire wasn't just directed at Molly. She could have been any woman, and he'd have reacted the same.

Or would he? Molly had been sassy on the mountain trail. And she'd been very convincing about not calling in the authorities. She was strong and determined.

He could almost bet she'd have found a way off the mountain without his help. Still, he was glad that theory hadn't been tested.

Kujo closed his eyes, hoping that by not staring at the beautiful woman, he could almost forget how close their bodies were.

Ha! Closing his eyes only made him more aware of the softness of her curves and the peachy scent of her hair.

The night promised to be a long one. As he lay awake, sleep the furthest thing from his mind, he thought through Molly's responses to his questions. He knew she was lying, but he couldn't figure out why.

As soon as the sun came up, he'd go after the drone. Perhaps he could see what the camera had recorded to know better what Molly was really up to, and what someone didn't want her to find.

The longer he lay with Molly curled against him, the sleepier he got and his desire slowly ebbed.

When he opened his eyes again, the gray light of pre-dawn filled the windows. He tried to move his arm, but couldn't and turned to see why.

Molly lay in the crook of his arm, her cheek resting on his chest. Her auburn hair spread out in wild abandon, the fiery strands tickling his nose.

The blanket had slipped behind her, leaving her legs bare, one silken calf curled over his leg, her knee resting against his crotch.

His usual morning erection sprang to attention.

Sweet Jesus, he had to get up quickly or risk frightening the poor woman with a monster boner.

He edged away, slipping his arm out from under her, in such a hurry, he rolled out of the bed backwards and landed on the ground on top of Six.

The dog yelped and skittered out of the way.

"What the hell?" a groggy voice said from above.

Kujo pushed to his feet. "Sorry, I was trying not to wake you."

"I'm not awake," she assured him. She blinked her eyes and pushed the hair out of her face. "Are you okay?"

Hell, no. He was hard and had no way to relieve the

need. No, he wasn't okay. "Yeah. I have some beef jerky, if you're hungry, and a can of beans."

"I'll pass." Molly stretched and winced. "I found some more sore spots. I don't suppose you have another one of those pain pills."

"I do. But you should eat something before you take it."

"Jerky, then. And water." She licked her lips.

The movement made his stomach flip crazily. Kujo turned away before his arousal became evident. He reached into his duffel bag for the snack, tore the package open and handed a strip of dried beef to Molly.

She accepted his offering, ripped off a piece with her teeth and chewed with her eyes closed. "I feel like I was put through a meat grinder."

"You took a pretty serious tumble." He handed her a bottle of water he'd had in his bag.

She leaned up on her elbow and drank deeply. When she'd slaked her thirst, she capped the bottle and sat it on the nightstand. "I need to find the drone." Molly swung her legs over the edge of the bed and winced again.

"You need to stay put," Kujo said. "You aren't up to dodging bullets, just yet."

"I'm not going to be ready to dodge anything by lying around being waited on."

"Seriously, I saw your drone go down. I'll find what's left of it and bring it back. Besides, there's only one four-wheeler, and the handlebars are bent."

Molly bit her lip. "I wonder what that's going to cost me when I turn it into the rental place." She shook her head. "If you were able to steer it and carry me back, I should be able to manage it." She sat up and pressed a hand to her ribs. "Did you see the mule that kicked me?"

A smile tugged at the corners of his mouth. The woman was far too independent for her own good. "You're not going anywhere. It wasn't easy getting you here on that four-wheeler. I don't relish doing it again should something happen out there."

"I can take care of myself." She gave him a sheepish grin. "For the most part. But thank you for taking care of me." When she tried to get out of the bed, Six stood in front of her.

"See? Even the dog doesn't want you to leave."

"Look, I can't leave that drone out there. It's an expensive piece of equipment."

He held out one of the pills he'd given her the night before. "Take this. It'll help with the aches and pains."

"I'm not changing my mind." Molly bent forward, determined to get up. As soon as she leaned toward him, her face creased in a grimace, and she eased back. "Seriously, did you get that mule's number?"

"Will you stop acting tough and take the damned pill?" He took her hand and placed the medication on her palm.

"What is it, anyway?" she asked and then placed it on her tongue and washed it down with the water.

"It's one of the painkillers my doctor gave me."

"Strong stuff."

His jaw tightened. "Needed to be."

"Do you still take it?" Her gaze slipped down his body to his legs.

Kujo didn't want pity. He could get around almost as well as before the injury. Yes, it was more painful, but he didn't let that stop him, and he didn't rely on the drugs. Too many of the wounded warriors lost their lives to drugs, alcohol and suicide. He wasn't going to be one of them. "Not often. I didn't want to get hooked."

Molly nodded. "Well, thanks. But I have a feeling you gave me that pill to keep me here. The last one knocked me out." She bit into another piece of the jerky and chewed.

"You almost died. Give yourself time to recuperate." He turned and opened the door for Six.

While the animal was outside, Kujo slipped on his boots and stoked the fire to chase away the chill of the morning air.

"Joe?" Molly called out.

"Yes?" He looked over his shoulder at her, sitting with her back to the wall, the blanket covering her sexy legs. He wanted to crawl back into the bed with her. In the light of day, he was almost positive she would put up a fight.

"I had a dream last night." Her cheeks reddened.

His heartbeat sputtered and sped up. "Yeah?"

"I dreamed I was falling down that hill again."

"I'm sure you did." He closed the door on the stove. "Something like that is hard to get over."

"Joe?"

He had nothing else to fiddle with and was forced to face the woman lying in his bed, her wild hair and makeup-less face not at all detracting from her appearance. In fact, she looked like a woman who'd just had sex.

Holy shit. Where had that thought come from? He sure as hell didn't need to think down those lines. He'd just gotten his hard-on under control. Further, she'd be out of his cabin and out of his life as soon as they figured out who shot at her and her drone.

The red in her cheeks deepened, and she looked down at where her fingers were pulling at the fabric of the blanket. "When I was falling...in my dream... someone caught me."

Kujo's gut clenched. "And?"

Molly glanced up at him. "It was you, wasn't it?"

His groin tightened, recalling how she'd felt snuggled up against him throughout the night. He forced a casual shrug. "I don't know. I wasn't in your dream. I don't read minds."

"No, but you held me in the night, didn't you?" Her brows pulled together. "You were my dream catcher, weren't you?"

He couldn't lie. "You were having a bad dream and moaning. All I did was hold you until it was over." Okay, that last part might have been stretching the truth. He'd held her all night, until he fell out of the bed.

Molly nodded. "I thought I was still dreaming. Not the nightmare, but a good dream. And you were warm when I was cold." She smiled. "Thank you."

He turned away and opened the door for Six to come in. "No problem. And don't worry, I didn't do anything to violate you." Oh, he'd wanted to, but he wouldn't have. Not without her consent.

Her warm chuckle filled the interior of the little cabin. "It's nice to know chivalry is alive and well in the Crazy Mountains."

"I prefer my women conscious," he said.

She arched an eyebrow. "And I'd like to think I'd remember it if you'd tried something. But last night was a little foggy to me." Molly ran a hand through her hair, pushing it back from her face.

The movement drew Kujo's attention to the T-shirt as it stretched across her breasts. He could see the black lace through the white fabric and wanted to unclip the back again and do more than rub ointment into her wounds.

MOLLY STARED AT KUJO, noting the way his nostrils flared whenever she moved. The man was a complete stranger. He could have done anything to her during the night, and no one would have been the wiser.

But he hadn't.

She was at once delighted to know she could trust him, while disappointed he hadn't even tried to squeeze one of her breasts or cup her sex.

Her core tightened, and an ache grew between her legs. She pulled the blanket up a little higher to cover her from the waist down.

The man couldn't help he was hot and sexy. She found it hard to believe he'd been in the bed with her and she hadn't been awake enough to do anything about it. She wanted to ask for a do-over so she might snuggle even closer and maybe taste his skin and touch him in some of his naughty places.

Heat filled her cheeks and rushed all the way out to the tips of her ears. She had to pull her mind out of the gutter, and quickly. The man was a loner, and she was invading his space. As soon she felt up to leaving, she would.

She yawned, covering her mouth with her hand. "Damned pills knock me out."

"Then sleep. I'll be back in a little while."

"I want to…" she yawned again, "come with you."

"You'll fall off the four-wheeler if you do."

She tilted her chin. "Not if you hold onto me."

He shook his head. "No. It's too dangerous—even when you're not drugged."

She yawned again and tipped over onto the pillow. "If you insist. But don't let anyone shoot at you. I kinda like having you around." Molly closed her eyes. "I'll only be asleep for a little while. When I wake up, I can help…"

"Rest." His warm, rich voice coated her like chocolate syrup. "I'm leaving Six with you."

"That's nice," she muttered and patted the side of the bed. "Come here, boy."

Molly registered the sound of the dog's toenails clicking across the floor. Six nudged her hand, pushing his head beneath it.

Molly scratched him behind his ears, and then patted the mattress beside her.

The dog eased up into the bed and stretched out, resting his furry body against hers.

"Traitor," Kujo said.

Molly peeked from beneath her heavy eyelids. "He likes me."

"You're going to be hell on my retraining efforts."

"Dogs were meant to be loved," she said, wrinkling her nose and slipping her arm around Six's neck.

"I'll be back as soon as possible. Don't go anywhere."

"Oh, I'm not. And when I wake up, I'll be as good as new," Molly promised.

The door creaked open, sending a cool blast of mountain air into the warm cabin. As quickly as it opened, it closed again, leaving Molly and Six in silence.

"I hope he'll be all right," Molly said and snuggled against Six, falling into a deep sleep.

CHAPTER 9

FOR A LONG MOMENT, Kujo stood outside the cabin, hesitant to leave Molly alone, but unwilling to take her with him when she was still in pain from her injuries. Besides, she'd slow him down if he had to beat a hasty retreat.

He had no idea how he'd ended up in the same place at the same time as she had two days ago, but his gut told him he'd been there for a reason. He was glad the reason was to save Molly. She was bright, strong and beautiful. When he got back from searching for the drone, he'd get the truth out of her. If not by force, then by other, more pleasurable means.

With a sense of urgency, he climbed onto the four-wheeler, started the engine and roared away, back the direction he'd come when he'd held an unconscious woman in his arms, trying not to drop her while steering the damaged vehicle.

The bent steering wheel took some getting used to

again, but he didn't let it slow him on his quest to find the drone.

As he approached the ridge, he slowed the four-wheeler to a stop and killed the engine. He'd go the rest of the way on foot. Whoever had been in the valley might still be there, and he intended to find out who it was.

After hiding the four-wheeler in the brush, he slipped through the woods and up to the top of the ridge, clinging to the shadows of the trees and under-brush. He stood for a long moment, scanning the valley below. As far as he could see, nothing moved. The caves dotting the cliffs on the opposite side stared back at him like gaping maws, so dark he couldn't see into them. A single, narrow road led in from the eastern end of the valley. If he hadn't been studying it so carefully, he might have missed it.

Before he started down the ridge, he studied the area where he recalled the drone had gone down. Aiming for that location, Kujo slipped over the edge of the ridge and down through the trees toward the valley floor. He moved as quietly as he could on the steep slope, step-ping over twigs and taking care not to slip on the gravel.

When he reached the bottom, he slipped through the woods, shadow to shadow, until he came to an opening, bright with sunlight and green grass. A creek ran through the valley, burbling over rocks, reflecting sparkles of sunshine. Nothing about the setting screamed danger, but Kujo didn't let down his guard. He studied the forest glen, hoping to spot something white or shiny, like parts to the drone Molly had been operating.

On the opposite side of the creek something glinted on the gravel banks. He focused on the spot. The wind shifted, tossing tree branches over the banks, allowing another patch of light to hit that area. Again, something bright shined in the dull gravel.

His pulse quickening, Kujo made his way along the banks of the creek, searching for a crossing point that wouldn't leave him exposed for very long. He found a point where the stream narrowed and the trees formed an arch, shadowing the banks and the water. After studying both directions and glancing up at the dark cave entrances, he hurriedly leaped over the water and ducked back into the shadows.

Moving quickly, he reached the spot where the shiny object lay. It was part of the drone. He left it where it was for the moment and searched the surrounding area. Piece by piece, he located the rest of the drone. The main body of the device was still intact; two of the arms had snapped off in the crash landing. A hole through the center marked the spot where a bullet had gone through the motor.

Kujo doubted the drone would fly again, but he'd carry it back and see if they could salvage the camera or the disk that stored the video data. He piled the parts in one location against the base of a tree, hiding it in the brush, and then looked up at the caves.

Part of him wanted to get back to the cabin in a hurry, fearing someone could have traced him and

Molly there. But something about the caves made him stay. What was someone hiding in the valley? He hadn't seen anything other than trees, boulders and the stream on the valley floor. The narrow road leading in could have been an old mining road used back in the days when men mined the mountains for gold and silver. Hunters might still use it during hunting season. The road ran the length of the valley following the base of the cliffs with the caves.

Someone with a need to keep things on the downlow could have used the road to run people or supplies into the valley. Perhaps they'd used the caves to store supplies.

Or teenagers could have used the road and the caves for campouts and parties where they'd be out of sight and range of concerned parents.

Either way, Kujo felt the need to explore the caves before he left the valley.

Choosing the least revealing path up to the largest and most accessible cave entrance, he crossed the road and eased up the side of the rise. He didn't know what he would find, man, beast or nothing at all, but he'd be prepared for anything. Except maybe a bear. For a bear, he'd need a bigger gun.

The last few yards up to the entrance were traversed in the open. He had no other choice but to make a run for it, up the hill and into the darkness, without knowing what to expect. Taking a deep breath, he sprinted up the incline, his bad leg aching with the effort. He ignored the pain and ducked into the shadows, then stood with his back to the cave wall. Listening, he stared into the darkness, his heart thundering all the while. God, he'd missed the game of hide and seek with the enemy. Pitting his strengths against the Taliban or ISIS had always been an adrenaline high.

Slowly, his vision adjusted to the dimly lit interior. It appeared like any other cave with a stone floor and a damp, earthy smell. Since nothing moved, Kujo ventured deeper inside. At the very back, he had to use the tiny flashlight he kept in his pocket. He shined the narrow beam along the walls and floors. In a corner, he found what appeared to be the remains of a wooden crate with military identification markings on it.

Kujo frowned, broke off the part with the writing painted on it and hurried back to the entrance. Again, nothing moved that he could see. The valley was almost eerily silent. Even the birds paused in their songs.

When he was certain the coast was clear, Kujo climbed down the trail to the road below and hurried to the next cave. It wasn't as deep, but it had a small scorched area where someone had set up a campfire. Based on the charred remains, it appeared to have been in the recent past with a fresh stash of tinder tucked in the driest area of the cave. From this cave's position, he could see across the entire valley. It was a good vantage point for a lookout, or a machine gunner.

The next two caves proved to be smaller still and barely cut back into the mountain. By the time he finished exploring them, he'd been gone from the cabin for over two hours. He didn't like leaving Molly that long. As far as he could tell, the valley was empty. Which led to the next question. Where was the shooter?

Kujo jogged across the valley floor to where he'd left the drone parts, gathered them in his arms, along with the board from the crate, and hurried up the hillside and over the top of the ridge. He made it to the ATV without running into anyone or being the target of a shooter.

Though he was glad he'd been danger-free, he couldn't help feeling he should be back at the cabin by now. His gut was telling him to hurry.

He piled his collection into the basket on the front of the four-wheeler, slung his leg over the seat and started the engine. It sputtered and died.

Sweet Jesus! Not now. He held his breath and hit the starter switch again. The engine chugged, and then caught and roared. Letting out the breath he'd held, he raced back toward the cabin.

SUN SHONE through the windows of the cabin when Molly opened her eyes again. She pushed to a sitting position, only mildly discomfited by the twinge in her ribs. The additional, dreamless sleep had left her refreshed and ready to face the world.

Six yawned, stretched and stepped down off the bed where he continued to stretch, until he ended his routine with a hearty shake.

Molly wished she could do the same and be ready to rock and roll. Instead, she swung her legs over the edge of the bed and stood. Aches and pains made her stiff, but the painkiller Joe had given her dulled her suffering to a manageable level. She stretched carefully, babying her ribs. She needed to relieve herself and find some water to splash on her face.

Six stood beside the door, expectantly.

"You, too?" She opened the door for the dog and stepped out onto the porch.

The mountain air hit her legs and forced her back inside where she slipped into her jeans. She didn't try to put on her shirt, noticing it was shredded on the back where she'd slid down the hillside. Joe's shirt would have to suffice for the time being. She lifted the fabric to her nose and sniffed. It still smelled like him, clean, fresh and woodsy.

She sat in one of the two wooden chairs the cabin sported and pulled on her boots. Her 9-millimeter lay on the table where Joe had left it. She slipped the holster over her shoulders and gingerly settled it in place over the cuts and scrapes Joe had so carefully bandaged.

As much as she liked to think she could take care of herself, she couldn't have treated her own wounds. Joe had been a perfect gentleman when he'd cleaned them, smeared ointment and applied the dressings. What if he hadn't been so platonic? What if he'd smoothed his hand over her unaffected skin and twisted his fingers in her hair?

A tremor rippled through Molly. The man was every woman's dream: tall, dark and ruggedly handsome with broad shoulders and thick muscles. Lying against him through the night had left her feeling safe and protected.

Of course, that wasn't what a good FBI special agent should need. So far, her first field assignment was an unmitigated disaster. She didn't have any more information than she'd started with, and she'd crashed a very expensive drone. Molly dreaded the call she'd have to make to her supervisor when she got back to town. He'd likely order her to return to DC and her desk job.

As far as Molly was concerned, the threat of returning to boring background checks was all the more reason to hold off on that call until she could dig a little deeper and find where the ISIS training was being conducted. What a coup that would be. If she could pull that off, maybe her boss wouldn't be so angry about the drone. And she might get more field assignments.

If she proved herself a competent field agent, she'd request a transfer out of DC to one of the regional offices. She wondered if they had one in Montana. She was quickly falling in love with the mountains and the wide-open plains. And the male scenery wasn't so bad, either.

Not that she was in Montana to start a relationship. Her track record in that department sucked. Still... Joe was a temptation she might not be able to resist. Perhaps a fling was in order to tamp down her desires and hold her for a while.

Her core tingled at the thought of giving in to a little mattress dancing with the former soldier. Based on how gently he'd treated her wound, Molly bet Joe would be an amazing lover.

In the meantime, she had to pee. Six stood by a tree with one leg hiked. Seeing him relieving himself, made

Molly's needs even more urgent. She rounded the cabin hoping to find an outhouse. No such luck. The cabin had to have been built for male hunters with no regard to a female's requirements. Hiking out into the trees, she found a spot in the shadows and took care of business. The gurgling sound of running water lured her deeper into the woods.

Six caught up, passed her and led the way to a pretty stream, nestled in a copse of trees. Molly followed the stream a little way and found where it widened into a pool, big enough to swim in. What a heavenly place, and what a change from the city streets and traffic of her home back on the east coast. Why would anyone want to leave the Crazy Mountains of Montana?

The air was cool, but the sun found its way through the trees to the pool, making it shine like glass. Molly turned in a three-hundred-sixty-degree circle. She would bet there wasn't a soul within miles of where she stood.

Before she could change her mind, she shucked her boots, stripped out of her clothes and peeled off the bandages she could reach. After sliding down a hill, she was still covered in dirt. A dip in the pool would go a long way toward reviving her spirit and washing away the dirt.

When she was completely naked, she dipped a foot into the water. *Holy moly!* It was icy cold. Knowing there was only one way to get clean, she dove in and surfaced, her breath frozen in her chest. Wow, it was cold.

Six stood on the bank, lapping at the water.

Molly laughed. "Now who's the more intelligent species?"

Six looked up and sat, prepared to wait for her to get out of the water. He stood guard while Molly worked the dust out of her hair and off her skin. At first the water stung her wounds, but after a minute or two, the cold numbed them, as well as her feet and toes. She finished quickly and climbed the banks, refreshed and feeling almost normal.

The cool air felt warm after the chill of the water. She stood in the sunshine, squeezing the excess water from her hair and shaking her arms and legs until they dried enough for her to dress. Still damp, she slipped into her jeans and Joe's shirt, pulled on her boots and slipped her holster in place.

When she straightened, a breeze blew through the trees, bringing with it the acrid scent of smoke.

Six paced in front of her as she buckled her shoulder holster and pulled on her jacket. The smoke seemed to be coming from the direction of the cabin.

Molly took off running. Her ribs hurt with every footfall. She ignored the pain and raced through the woods, emerging in the clearing to find the cabin in flames.

Had she left the door open to the potbellied stove? How could it be so consumed in flames when she'd only been gone for less than half an hour?

A movement caught her eye around the side of the building. A man wearing a ski mask slung liquid at the side of the cabin from a red jug. The pungent scent of gasoline filled the air as flames licked at the wooden sides of the structure.

"Hey!" Molly yelled and raced toward the man.

The bastard was pouring gasoline on the cabin.

Six streaked past her and reached him first to sink his teeth into the man's arm.

The man yelled and kicked at the dog in an attempt to free his arm.

Six refused to let go, his body swinging around with the man's movements.

Molly pulled her weapon and aimed at the man, but was afraid to shoot and injure the dog.

Finally, the man's shirt ripped off his arm, and Six fell to the ground. Before the dog could latch onto him again, the man ran around to the other side of the cabin.

Molly raced after him, but didn't catch up before he sped away in an old red and white pickup. She ran down the road after it, hoping to get the license plate number, but the vehicle didn't have one.

Six chased the truck around the bend in the dirt road, leading toward the highway.

"Six!" Molly yelled. She didn't want the dog hurt by the arsonist, or for him to get hit on the highway. She sprinted after him, her heart pounding against her chest. As she reached the curve in the road, Six appeared, trotting toward her.

Molly slowed to a stop and bent over, breathing hard. The fire raged behind her. Once she filled her lungs, she went back to see what she could do to contain the damage.

The cabin was completely engulfed in flames, and

the heat intense. Molly couldn't get inside to salvage any of Joe's belongings.

Embers flew into the air, landing on pine straw and starting up smaller fires in the immediate vicinity.

Molly hurried to stamp down the flames of the smaller fires, afraid the blaze would spread to the woods beyond and set that whole damned forest on fire.

CHAPTER 10

HALFWAY BACK TO THE CABIN, Kujo topped a hill and froze.

A plume of smoke billowed into the air from the direction of the cabin.

Damn! He knew he shouldn't have left Molly alone in the cabin. And he'd given her a painkiller.

His heart in his throat, he raced down the hill and through the woods as fast as the damaged four-wheeler would carry him. Every horrible scenario he could imagine raced through his mind. Molly could be trapped in the cabin. By the time he reached her, there'd be nothing left but her charred remains. And Six...

Fuck! Why couldn't the ATV move any faster? As it was, he nearly crashed into a boulder at one bend in the trail and narrowly missed a tree trunk at another. When he finally emerged into the clearing around the cabin, his heart sank to his knees. The cabin was a complete loss, the flames licking the sky, smoke chugging into the air in billowing puffs.

If Molly hadn't gotten out…

Kujo brought the ATV to a skidding stop, leaped off and ran around the side of the building, racing for the entrance.

The porch roof had collapsed blocking the door. Even if he'd wanted to go inside, he couldn't.

He stood staring at the inferno, his chest squeezing so tightly he couldn't breathe.

A hand touched his arm, and he nearly jumped out of his skin.

"Joe?"

He spun to find Molly standing behind him with Six at her heels. "Oh, dear God." He pulled her into his arms and crushed her to his chest. "I thought you were still inside."

She wrapped her arms around his waist and leaned her cheek against his chest. "We're okay, but I'm afraid your cabin is toast."

"I don't give a damn about the cabin." He buried his face in her hair for another long moment before he lifted his head.

Molly looked up at him, her brow furrowed. "We should probably move away from the fire, before we become a part of it."

Without releasing Molly all the way, Kujo walked her away from the blaze and bent to scratch Six's ears. He cleared a lump in his throat before he spoke. "I though you two were inside," he said, his voice hoarse.

"We were in the woods when it started." Molly touched a hand to his cheek. "We're fine, but Joe, someone set this fire."

"What do you mean?" He jerked his head up and looked around. "Who?"

"I don't know. He wore a ski mask and took off in an old red and white pickup. He used gasoline as an accelerant."

"Bastard," Kujo said.

"No kidding." Molly shook her head. "Six tried to stop him, but he got away. He should have some significant bite marks on his right arm. Six was amazing."

Kujo ruffled Six's neck, and then hugged Molly close again. "I'm just glad you weren't inside."

Molly stared up at him. "You were really worried?" She stepped back and stared at him. "Joe, you're shaking."

He closed his eyes, the images of those soldier's faces permanently etched in his mind as the world exploded around them. "I couldn't go through that again," he whispered.

She cupped his cheek. "Through what?"

The sound of sirens gave Kujo the needed distraction from confessing his own nightmares. "That will be the fire department. You need to hide if you want to remain missing."

Molly shook her head. "Whoever set the fire knows I'm here. There's no point remaining in hiding."

"Good, then as soon as they have the blaze under control, I'm taking you to my boss."

"Your boss?" She stared up at him, her brows dipping.

A short fire truck bumped up the road toward them, followed by a longer one and a tanker truck filled with water. Pickup trucks lined the drive as volunteer fire-fighters pulled in and jumped out, ready to assist and put the flames out before the flames spread and created a forest fire.

Kujo moved the four-wheeler out of the way. Then he and Molly loaded the drone parts into his pickup and parked the truck farther along the road, out of the way of the firefighters.

Within the hour, they had the fire contained in a smoldering pile of ash that once was a hunting retreat in the woods.

Kujo stood with Molly in the curve of his arm, watching as the experts dealt with the fire. The sheriff showed up with a couple of his deputies to ask questions.

Molly told him what she'd witnessed.

"You didn't see his face at all?" the sheriff asked as he made notes on a pad.

"No, sir," Molly answered. "He wore a ski mask and took off in an ancient red and white pickup."

The sheriff's eyes narrowed. "Not many red and white pickups around these parts anymore."

One of the deputies leaned toward the sheriff. "Doesn't Old Man Donovan have an antique hunk of junk pickup?"

The sheriff nodded and scribbled a note on the page. "Notify dispatch to send someone out to check on Donovan and his truck."

The deputy hustled toward his vehicle to do the sheriff's bidding.

The sheriff locked gazes with Kujo. "You know, Ray

Diener blames you for his wife leaving him. You sure you didn't see him?"

Kujo shook his head. "Molly was here alone. But whoever did it will have a nasty dog bite on his arm."

The sheriff shot a glance at Six. "He's not dangerous, is he?"

"He's a trained war dog," Kujo said. "But Six was mostly used for bomb sniffing."

Sheriff Barron reached down to scratch Six's ears. "Hopefully, he won't have much bomb sniffing to do around here."

"He's retired from service." Kujo glanced toward the men rolling up hoses. "Are you done with us?"

"For now," the sheriff said. "Will you be in the area for long?"

"Yes, sir. Now that the cabin's gone, I'll have to get a place in town."

"Good. I might have more questions as we get further along in the investigation." The sheriff stared at the smoldering heap. "Could have been worse. You're lucky no one was inside when he lit the place."

Kujo's chest tightened all over again. "Yes, sir."

Sheriff Barron's gaze swept the surroundings. "And had the fire burned out of control, it could have wiped out thousands of acres. We'll do what we can to put the arsonist away."

"Thank you, sir," Molly said.

Kujo cupped her elbow and led her away from the firefighters as they cleaned up. When he reached his truck, he helped her up into the passenger side and opened the back door for Six. After the dog jumped into the back seat, Kujo closed the door, rounded the front of the vehicle and slipped into the driver's seat.

"Where to?" Molly asked, fastening her seatbelt.

"To Hank Patterson's place."

"He's your boss?"

Kujo nodded.

Six stuck his head between the seats and stared out the front window.

"What kind of work do you do?" Molly turned to pet Six.

Kujo shrugged. "Security work, from what I can tell."

"You don't know?"

"I just signed on. I haven't had my first assignment. You can ask him when we get there."

Molly settled back in her seat. "Is he prior military as well?"

"SEAL."

Molly's brows rose. "And you're former Delta Force?" She smiled his way. "The best-of-the-best. Does he hire all former spec-ops-trained personnel?"

"As far as I know."

"Interesting. I look forward to meeting him. Where does he live?"

"On White Oak Ranch. His wife is Sadie McClain."

Molly shot a glance his way. "*The* Sadie McClain? Hollywood phenomenon?"

Kujo frowned. "I suppose."

"Now, I'm really interested in meeting them." She shook her head. "Wow, I came to Montana thinking I'd just meet backwoods and small-town folk. I didn't expect to meet Sadie McClain."

The rest of the trip to White Oak Ranch passed in silence.

When they pulled up to the ranch house, Hank, Duke, Bear and three other men rose from chairs on the porch and came down the steps to greet them.

"Kujo, I'm glad you're here. I was just about to send someone out to get you from that hunting cabin." Hank held out his hand. "You have to move to a place with phone service. In the meantime, I'll equip you with a satellite phone and a GPS tracker."

"Hank, Bear, Duke." Kujo shook hands with the men he knew and turned to the others.

Hank clapped his shoulder and turned to the other men. "Men, this is Joseph Kuntz, or more affectionately known as Kujo. Kujo meet Axel Svenson, Brandon Rayne and Vince Van Cleave. Alex Davila is on assignment. Actually, all these men are on assignment, but came in for a brief meeting."

Kujo held out his hand to the big Viking of a man with blond hair and blue eyes.

Axel grinned. "They call me Swede."

Kujo nodded, and then shook hands with a broad-shouldered, man with black hair and gray eyes.

"My parents named me Brandon, but my SEAL team called me Boomer."

"Which do you prefer?" Kujo asked.

Brandon lifted his chin. "Boomer."

Molly chuckled. "Do any of you go by your real names?" She turned to Kujo. "I'll have to remember that. Cujo was a killer dog, right?"

He shook his head. "Nothing that impressive. It's

short for Kuntz, Joseph." He cupped her elbow and guided her forward. "Hank, this is Molly Greenbriar."

Hank grinned. "So, *you're* Miss Greenbriar." He held out his hand.

Molly took it, her brows furrowing. "Should I know you?"

"Not at all. I got word from a buddy of mine in the FBI that you'd be in the area. Pete Ralston. Know him?"

Kujo shot a narrow-eyed glance at Molly. "FBI?"

She gave him a sheepish half-grin. "I was supposed to be flying under the radar. You know, incognito." She shook her head and faced Hank. "Pete's my supervisor."

"He asked that I keep an eye out for you. That you were doing some surveillance work."

Anger roiled in Kujo's gut. He didn't like it when he was left out of the information loop. "Apparently, she was doing surveillance work—until someone shot her drone out of the sky and tried to kill her."

Hank's brows rose. "Is that so?" He studied her. "Is that why you're covered with soot? Are you all right?"

"We just came from Joe's cabin," she said. "Someone torched it."

Hank shook his head. "Okay. You two need to fill me in on what's going on." He climbed the stairs and entered the house. "Sadie? We have more company!"

Kujo let Molly go first. As she passed him, he whispered, "Thanks for letting me in on the joke."

"No joke. Just what my supervisor ordered," she said. "Apparently, the cat's out of the bag. At least with Hank and his organization."

He followed her, and Six trailed behind them,

entering the house with the big group of Brotherhood Protectors.

Molly's words didn't make Kujo feel any better about being left out of the loop. He'd have a long discussion with her later and get all the pertinent facts.

"Oh!" Sadie McClain stood in the middle of the large living area, a baby on her hip. "I didn't realize you had *female* company. What a pleasant change."

Molly stood in awe of one of her favorite actresses.

The woman graced the silver screen in multiple movies that had shot to the top of the ratings. She could demand any salary she wanted, and there she stood in faded blue jeans, her gorgeous blond hair up in a casual, messy bun and baby spit up on the shoulder of her T-shirt.

She laughed, her blue eyes twinkling as she looked down at her mussed appearance. "Pardon my mess. I was awake most of the night with Emma. She's teething. We just got up from a much-needed two-hour nap."

"Don't let me interrupt. I'm sure you have plenty to do without playing hostess to an army of people in your living room," Molly said. She stepped up to the woman and baby. "I'm Molly Greenbriar."

"Are you another one of Hank's new recruits?" She nodded toward Kujo. "I've met Kujo and Boomer. I didn't know he'd hired a female. I think that's awesome."

"No, no. I have a job. I just happened to...run into Joe—Kujo, in the woods a couple days ago."

Kujo stepped up beside her. "Could I?" he held out his hands for the baby.

"Sure." Sadie handed him the baby then bent to scratch behind Six's ears. "Hey, Six." She glanced up. "Oh, be forewarned, Emma just ate, and she tends to burp with projectile vomit."

Kujo held the baby away from him, raising her up and down without holding her against his body. "On second thought, you'd better take her." He handed the baby back to Sadie.

"Don't have the stomach for baby vomit?" Sadie grinned. "No worries. Neither did I before I had Emma. It's amazing what you learn to tolerate when you love someone as much as we love this little pooping, puking machine." She rubbed noses with Emma, making her giggle.

"No, I just remembered I smell like smoke," Kujo said. "I didn't want to share that with the baby."

Sadie frowned. "Camping out?"

Molly snorted. "I wish that were the reason."

Hank joined them. "The hunting cabin Kujo was staying in burned to the ground."

Sadie's eyes widened. "Wow. I hope no one was hurt." She stared from Kujo to Molly. "That would explain the smudged look. I wondered if it was a fashion statement." She balanced Emma on her hip, grabbed Molly's hand and said, "Come with me. I can fix you up with something clean to wear until you can get to your own clothes."

"I'm fine for now. I won't be here very long." She gave Hank a questioning look.

"Stay for as long as you need to. You're welcome to spend the night if necessary."

"No. I have a room at the B&B in town. And my clothes are all there." She tipped her head toward Joe—she'd never get used to calling him Kujo. "Kujo's the one who lost everything in the fire."

Hank eyed Kujo. "I have some jeans and shirts you can borrow until you can stock up on what you need. And you can stay with us until you find a place of your own."

"I'll stay at the B&B in town," he said. "If they have a spare room…"

Molly's heart fluttered at the news. She'd see more of Joe than just the past two days. "I would like to use the facilities in the meantime to wash my hands and face. I promise not to leave a mess."

"Honey, don't worry about it. I can't believe you two have been through the trauma of a fire." She turned. "Follow me."

Molly fell in step behind the gorgeous actress, pinching herself inside, when all she wanted to do was fangirl all over Sadie McClain.

Sadie showed her to the bathroom on the main level and left her with a fresh towel. "Think you can find your way to the kitchen when you're done? I'm sure the men will be gathered around the table in there. Just follow the noise."

After scrubbing her face and hands, Molly finger-combed her hair and grimaced at her reflection in the mirror. So much for swimming in the pool earlier. She was a wreck. The sooner they made it back to the B&B, the better.

Taking a deep breath, she left the bathroom and followed the sound of deep, male voices to a huge kitchen equipped with state-of-the-art appliances. At one end was a table large enough to seat twenty people. With the seven men seated around it, Molly could see how useful it was.

The men quieted when she entered.

Kujo stood and pulled a seat out between him and Hank at the head of the table.

Molly sat. "Don't stop talking on my account."

"We were just chewing the fat while we waited for you to discuss what's happened since you came out to Montana." Hank laid his palms on the table. "Shoot."

Molly told him her side of what happened, and Kujo recounted his recollection.

Hearing his side again reminded her of how she owed her life to this man. Joe had saved her from hypothermia or being scavenged by animals.

"And just what is it you're looking for in your surveillance?" Hank asked. "Pete hinted at terrorists without coming right out and spilling the beans."

Molly stared around the room at the men before her.

Hank touched her arm. "If it makes you feel any better, we've all been involved with special operations so secret, even the President of the United States didn't know about them."

"Every man in this room has had a top-secret clearance. You can trust us," Duke said. He elbowed Bear in the side. "Well, maybe not Bear. After all, who can trust a bear?"

Bear punched him in the shoulder before facing Molly. "If you want our help, you have to trust us."

"Yeah." Kujo crossed his arms over his chest and held her gaze.

Molly nodded. "I got a tip from one of our computer hackers back at headquarters in DC that there might be a terrorist training camp in the mountains near the town of Eagle Rock. I'm here to determine if there's any credence to that intel." She drew in a deep breath and let it out. "I was to observe and report back. I'm not cleared to engage the target."

Kujo dropped his arms to the table. "They sent you out here alone?"

"Apparently not." She nodded toward Hank. "My supervisor called for backup with the Brotherhood Protectors. In case you've been disconnected with the news, there was another ISIS attack in DC. They're working that now. I got this gig because they didn't see it as a big threat."

Joe's eyebrows lowered in a fierce frown. "Holy crap, Molly. If there's a terrorist training camp here, that's a huge can of worms that could have gotten you killed, and no one would ever have found your body."

Molly lifted her chin. "I can take care of myself."

Kujo snorted. "Like you did when you threw yourself over a cliff to save your ass?"

"The shooter didn't hit me with his bullets," Molly argued, though she knew she didn't have a leg to stand on. She sighed. "I know. I wasn't expecting to hit pay dirt the first day out." Which clearly demonstrated her lack of experience. Perhaps she wasn't ready for field assignments, after all.

"At the very least, you should have had a partner," Hank said. He glanced past her to the man seated beside her. "Kujo, consider Molly your first assignment. You're to keep her safe while she performs her mission. And under no circumstances are you to engage the enemy."

"What if they start shooting at us first?" Kujo asked.

Hank nodded. "Correction: no circumstances except being fired on. In the meantime, I'll work with your guy back in DC to see if we can track down the source of your intel. Perhaps they can trace the IP address to a street address or a name."

"Good luck," Molly said. "The guy in our office couldn't, and he's an expert, dark web hacker."

Hank's lips curled on the corners. "I've got people."

Kujo pushed to his feet. "The day's still early. I want to hit a few stores. Much as I appreciate the loan of your jeans and T-shirts, I'd rather have my own."

Hank stood. "I understand. If you can't find what you need, you're welcome to raid my closet." He turned to Molly. "How many people know you're in town?"

"The B&B owner, and the guy I rented my four-wheeler from." She shrugged. "It was my attempt at a low profile."

"Kujo, you're still pretty new. Maybe you two can go undercover as a couple looking for a place to live. That would give you the perfect excuse to look all over the county and surrounding mountains."

Molly shook her head. "I don't know... I have my

room at the B&B. I didn't tell the lady I had a boyfriend or anything." The idea of pretending she and Kujo were a couple made a swarm of butterflies take off in her belly.

"You can tell her he just arrived in town to surprise you," Hank said. "Think about it. It might save you some trouble and give Kujo a plausible reason to stick around."

With a flutter in her belly, Molly nodded. "Now, if we're done here, I could use a shower and change of clothes. The day's still young, and I have a job to do."

"Not without me," Kujo reminded her.

"Much as I'd like to do this on my own, I'll gladly accept your help." She held out her hand to Hank. "Thanks."

"Don't thank me." Hank took her hand and held it in his. "Kujo happened to be in the right place at the right time. Be careful in the Crazy Mountains. They say you can get lost in there. And by lost, I mean someone can bury a body that'll never be found."

Joe glanced at Molly then turned to Hank. "While we're out searching for a training camp, could you get one of your people to look at the camera on the drone Molly was flying?"

Molly nodded. "I'd send it back to DC, but that would take too much time and it might get more damaged in transit."

"There might be some footage to explain why someone felt the need to knock it out of the sky."

"I'll see what I can do. Show me whatcha got." Hank and the others followed them out to Kujo's pickup.

Kujo handed them the pieces of the drone, pointing out the bullet hole through the motor.

Hank swore. "Not only did they hit it, they hit it where it counted. Dead center. I'll have my guys look at it. If there's any video to be salvaged, you and Molly will be the first to know."

"And while you're at it, I found a piece of a crate in a cave close to where the drone went down. It appears to have government nomenclature painted on it. Perhaps you can trace it back to its origin."

Molly stared at the slat. "You didn't tell me about that."

"I was a bit preoccupied by a fire," he reminded her.

She'd cut him some slack this time. After he'd nearly come unglued when he'd found her alive, she figured the board was the last thing on his mind until now.

Having discharged their findings, Kujo held the door for Six, then Molly and helped her into her seat. He shook hands with Hank, got in beside her and started the engine. As he shifted into gear, he shot a glance her way. "Ready to find a terrorist training camp?"

She nodded. "Hell, yeah."

His brows drew together. "Are you feeling up to it?"

"I'm sore, but I'll live." She squared her shoulders and stared at the road ahead. After nearly dying on her last trip into the mountains, she was even more determined to find the person who'd shot down the drone and to locate the training camp. Having Kujo along would be a bonus. He'd cover her six.

But pretending to be a couple? That might push her comfort level a little too far.

CHAPTER 11

"WHERE TO FIRST?" Kujo asked as they entered Eagle Rock.

"I would think you'd want to replace your personal items as soon as possible. I don't recall seeing a department store, but the feed store might carry denim jeans and shirts."

They stopped at the feed store. Just as Molly said, they carried a selection of jeans and chambray shirts. Kujo purchased three pairs of jeans, four chambray shirts, a white dress shirt, a dozen pairs of socks and seven T-shirts. He added a camouflage duffel bag to the pile and a pair of binoculars. After he paid for everything, he stuffed the items in the duffel bag.

"You'll have another T-shirt available after I wash the one I'm wearing," Molly pointed out.

"Keep it. You lost a shirt in that fire," he reminded her.

"I brought enough to last a couple weeks. I'll be fine."

They stopped at the grocery store and picked up

toiletries, a case of bottled water and a box of microwavable popcorn.

"The B&B serves breakfast and has microwaves in the rooms. Most of our meals will be eaten out," Molly warned.

She gave him directions.

"The B&B is a big house that's been converted into several rooms for rent, operated by Mrs. Kinner. She's a seventy-year-old woman who has the energy of someone half her age. And she insists on being called Mrs. K."

"Sounds like a real ball-buster."

"She is." Molly smiled. "With a heart of gold."

Molly entered the house first. "Mrs. K?"

A diminutive woman, who couldn't be over five feet tall, pushed through a swinging door into a large dining area equipped with bistro-style tables. "Molly, I'm so glad you're here. I was going to call the sheriff since I hadn't seen you in two days. Where were you?"

Molly smiled. "I'm sorry. I should have called to let you know that my...fiancé came and carried me out to a hunting cabin in the woods for some alone time." She winked, her smile fading. "Unfortunately, the cabin burned to the ground this morning."

"Oh, dear Lord." Mrs. K clutched Molly's arm. "You two weren't in it when the fire started, were you?"

"No, thank goodness. But since Joe is in town, do you have a room he can rent while he's here? He's also got a dog with him."

"Oh, honey, I'm not so old that I'm offended when

young couples sleep together before they're married. He's more than welcome to share your room."

Molly's eyes widened. "But—"

"Dog, you say?" Mrs. K looked past them. "Where is it?"

"He's on the porch," Kujo said.

"Well, let me see him. I love dogs, though Mr. K never let me have them in the house." She gave them a sly smile. "Since he passed, I allow guests to bring their dogs. It gives me the chance to enjoy them without committing to one. I have so much work to do around here, I doubt I'd have time to give to another being."

Kujo opened the front door. "Six, come."

The German Shepherd entered the house and sat at Kujo's feet.

Mrs. K stood back. "My, he's a big fellow." She looked up at Kujo. "Is he friendly?"

"You can pet him. He won't bite, unless I tell him to."

"Oh, I'm not certain I'm reassured." Mrs. K reached out to pet Six and smiled when he nudged her to keep it up. "Oh, he is a sweet fellow. He's more than welcome. Just let me get another towel. It's a good thing you two can share a room. With the cattle auction in town, I'm booked through the rest of this week until next Sunday." She talked as she headed up the stairs.

Kujo almost laughed at the stunned and slightly desperate expression on Molly's face. But he didn't. Instead, he hooked her elbow like a good fiancé and guided her up the stairs.

Mrs. K fished a fresh towel out of a linen cabinet.

"You'll want to freshen up, I'm sure. I'll leave you two alone."

"Thank you, Mrs. K," Kujo said to fill in Molly's silence.

The older woman started for the stairs.

"Oh, Mrs. K?" Kujo called out.

She turned. "Do you need some shampoo and soap?"

"No, thank you," Kujo gave the woman one of his killer smiles. "We like the Eagle Rock area and the surrounding mountains, so we'll be out a lot searching for a place to live. Just in case you get worried."

She grinned. "Thank you for the notice. And if you're looking for a land agent, David Perez is the most knowledgeable agent in the area. And I wouldn't go stomping around on other people's property without an appointment. Some people around here would just as soon shoot first and ask questions later."

"Thank you," Kujo said. "We'll check him out and get lined up for appointments."

Molly stuck her key into the lock and pushed open the door. Once she and Kujo were inside, she closed it and shook her head. "We have to find somewhere else for you and Six to stay."

"You heard Mrs. K. She's booked."

"Then we'll find another B&B."

"If this one is full, the others will be as well." Kujo took her hand. "Besides, I'm your sidekick, your partner. How can we work as a team when we're staying in two different places?"

"I don't know, but we can't sleep in the same bed."

He chuckled. "Why not? We did last night, and I didn't hear any complaints."

Molly opened her mouth, but nothing came out. Then she snapped it shut. "I'll be first in the shower. You can unpack. There's room in the closet and the bottom two drawers of the dresser." She grabbed a shirt and jeans from hangers in the closet, and panties and a bra from the drawer and scurried into the connecting bathroom.

Kujo's lips curled. If the flush of color in Molly's cheeks was any indication, she was worried about sleeping with him. He wondered if she was worried he'd take advantage of her this time, or if she was attracted to him and afraid to act on that attraction.

No matter what the case, he wasn't leaving her alone in the B&B. After coming back to the burning cabin, he couldn't leave her alone anywhere. His chest had hurt so badly, he'd felt like he was having a heart attack as he'd stared into the blaze, thinking Molly was trapped inside.

He pulled the jeans and shirts from the duffel bag and ripped the tags and stickers off, tossing them in the wastebasket. He preferred to wash clothes before wearing them, but that would take too much time. Molly would be ready to hit the ground running again as soon as she'd showered and dressed.

He hung the jeans and shirts in the closet for the moment, unwrapped his toiletries from their packaging then looked out the window at the main street running north and south through Eagle Rock.

In a community this small, he found it hard to

believe it could harbor an ISIS training camp. Who were they recruiting? Ranchers? Farmers? Businessmen or women?

His stomach rumbled, reminding him they hadn't had breakfast or lunch. The local diner would be a good place to kill two birds with one stone. They could eat and gather information from the locals.

Molly entered the room, carrying her dirty clothing. She'd dressed in a clean pair of dark jeans and a white button-down blouse. Her hair was brushed back from her forehead, the damp tresses lying in a neat sheath over her shoulders and down the middle of her back.

The woman didn't need makeup or high heels to appear sexy. The natural glow of her skin and the bright green of her eyes made her more appealing to Kujo than any other woman he'd ever dated.

"Your turn," Molly said. "I left some hot water for you."

"Thanks." He nodded toward her. "How are your wounds?"

She smiled. "Healing nicely, thanks to you."

He didn't offer to medicate them again, knowing he would be pushing his own limits if he did. Kujo entered the bathroom, shucked his clothes and ducked into the shower. He spent the next few minutes standing under the spray, washing the soot off his body and hair while trying not to think of Molly in the same shower, naked with the water running over her breasts and down her belly to the juncture of her thighs. He groaned and switched the water to cold.

"Are you all right in there?" Molly asked, her voice muffled by the door.

"I'm fine." Just fine, with a boner and desire he couldn't slake. He was working with Molly, not dating her. Giving in to lust would only complicate their task and take the focus off the real issue.

Despite the use of cold water, Kujo spent several minutes freezing before his erection dissipated. Quickly, before he could start thinking of a naked Molly again, he turned off the water, dried his body and dragged on the stiff jeans and shirt and headed out of the bathroom.

Molly wasn't in the bedroom and neither were Kujo's new jeans and shirts, nor his soot-covered clothing. When had she come into the bathroom to collect his soiled clothes?

The door to the room opened and Molly appeared. "I hope you don't mind, but I took your clothes to the laundry room. I got them started in the washer. Mrs. K offered to switch them to the dryer while we're out."

"Thanks." He pulled on the new socks and his boots. "I'm ready when you are."

"I'd like to stop at the realtor's and set up some appointments to see property in the area," Molly said.

"We can do that on the way to the diner. I don't know about you, but I'm hungry enough to eat a side of beef. And while we're there, we can ask the locals what people do for work around here."

Molly's brows scrunched. "Are you already looking for a new job? You just started with Hank."

Kujo shook his head. "No, I need to give this one a

chance before I start looking again. I'm looking for reasons a community would condone such a thing as a terrorist training camp. Some people must know it's here—at least, ones the group has recruited."

"Most people recruited into such organizations have issues," Molly agreed. "Low self-esteem, being fired from a job, trouble with the law and more. You're right, the job situation around here might have contributed to brainwashed targets." Molly's belly growled and she pressed a hand to her midsection. "And yes, stopping to eat would be good."

They left the room, Six trotting along behind them.

"The diner is only two blocks away," Kujo said. "Do you feel well enough to walk?"

She nodded.

Kujo took her hand. He liked the feel of her soft warm hand in his.

Molly glanced up.

"Our cover, remember?" he whispered. "Might as well look like we're together." She might not be on board with the idea, but Kujo was liking it all too much.

MOLLY'S PULSE hammered through her veins. Holding Joe's hand shouldn't have had that effect on her. Could he feel the rapid beat of her heart through her fingertips? Would he think she was excited by his touch? Well, she was. Far more than she should have been, having only known him for such a short time.

And they'd share a bed that night, unless Joe slept on

the floor. If not him, she could. Joe. Kujo. She was having a hard time calling him by his nickname.

Good Lord, she didn't need the distraction of lust getting in the way of her first field assignment. This was her job. The career she'd chosen, trained for and loved. She'd be damned if she sabotaged it due to a fling with a handsome Army veteran.

For the sake of their cover, she forced a smile onto her face and pretended to enjoy being with him. That part wasn't hard at all. The man had proven brave, gentle and solid. And those muscles...

There she went again!

She walked the two blocks in silence, afraid if she opened her mouth, some of her tumultuous thoughts would spill out, and she'd make a fool of herself.

Other than holding her through the night and holding her tight in front of the burning cabin, he hadn't shown a desire to go any further. Perhaps he wasn't all that into her. And she shouldn't care.

Outside the diner, Kujo gave Six a one-word command, "Stay."

Six sat beside the entrance, his gaze on Kujo as his master held the door for Molly.

The diner had a retro-fifties appearance, with checkered black and white tile flooring, chrome finishes and checkered tablecloths.

"Welcome to Al's Diner," a waitress called out. "Pick a seat, I'll be with you in a minute."

Molly chose a table in the middle of the room, the better to eavesdrop on other patrons. She sat with her back to the door, allowing Kujo the seat facing the entrance, so that he could have her back.

He held her chair until she sat then took the one across from her.

"Hi, I'm Daisy, I'll be your server." The waitress brought menus and two glasses of water and laid them on the table. She took their drink orders and disappeared. When she came back with coffee for them both, she smiled and set them on the table. "You two are new in town."

Molly nodded. "Yes, we are."

"Passing through or looking to stay a while?" Daisy pulled an order pad from her apron pocket and a pencil from behind her ear.

"We're looking for a home in the area," Kujo said. "I'm Joe, and this is my fiancée, Molly."

"Joe and Molly, so glad to see people my age moving into Eagle Rock, rather than leaving."

"Are young people leaving?" Molly prompted.

"Oh, sure. Most kids graduate high school and leave for the bigger cities to go to universities or find jobs." She stood with her pen poised over the pad. "What can I getcha?" Daisy took their orders then glanced up. "Oh, hi, Mr. Perez. Find a seat. I'll be with you in a minute." She looked back at Molly and Kujo. "If you need a good real estate agent, Mr. Perez is one of the best in town. He knows everything about every piece of property in the county."

"Now, Daisy, that's an exaggeration." A dark-haired, dark-skinned man, dressed in neatly ironed slacks and a polo shirt, stepped up to the table where Molly and

Kujo sat. "Hi, I'm David Perez."

Kujo stood and held out his hand. "Joe Kuntz." He nodded toward Molly. "My fiancée, Molly."

Molly's tummy did a backflip when Kujo called her his fiancée. She liked the sound of it too much. Pushing the thought aside, she squared her shoulders and took Perez's hand. "Is it true you're a real estate agent?"

"I am." He pulled a card from his pocket and handed it to her. "Are you looking for a place?"

"We are," Kujo said. "We're considering moving to Eagle Rock, but we'd like to see all it has to offer."

A big man with shaggy hair and a beard turned on his stool at the counter. "If you're coming for the job opportunities, you're in the wrong place."

"What do you mean?" Molly asked.

"Coal mines are laying off workers. Pipeline work is on hold, and we got more people out of work than there are jobs in ranching."

"I'm sorry to hear that," she said.

The bearded man's eyes narrowed. "You ain't looking for work, are you?"

Kujo held up his hands. "No. I'm an independent contractor and do most of my work out of state."

"Then why live here in Eagle Rock?"

Kujo shrugged. "Why not? I travel most of the time, and my fiancée is into photography. She likes it here." He smiled. "Don't worry. We're not here job hunting. Just property shopping."

The grizzled man continued to frown but turned his back to them, mumbling, "Damned outsiders with more money than brains are driving the prices of property up around here."

Perez shook his head and smiled at them. "Don't let George discourage you. Most people in the area are friendly."

"Yeah, most of those who didn't lose their jobs," George muttered, still with his back to them.

"If you want to look around the area, I have time this afternoon. It'll only take me an hour to set up some appointments," Perez said.

Molly beamed like a new bride. "Could you?"

"Of course." Perez pulled out his cell phone. "I'm here for lunch, then I'll head back to my office. You can meet me there. Anything in particular you're looking for?"

"Your office is fine." Kujo glanced at Molly. "My fiancée is an avid photographer and has fallen in love with the Crazy Mountains. We'd like to look at acreage up against the national forests near there."

Perez made a note on his cell phone. "Got it. I'll see you in an hour." He left them to sit at a table with another man whose back was to them.

"Okay, we have an agent." Kujo sat in time for Daisy to bring out their plates of sandwiches and fries.

"What George said about people being out of work..." The waitress shook her head. "It changes people."

"How so?" Molly asked.

Daisy looked down at her hands. "My boyfriend—I should say, ex-boyfriend—lost his job working the oil pipeline. One day, Tanner was making good money, and we were thinking about getting married, building a house and having kids." She looked out the window of the diner. "Then he was out of a job with no prospects and no other skills than what he'd learned on the pipeline. He looked for work, even took a job at Pinion Ranch doing manual labor."

"Wasn't *any* work better than none for him?" Molly asked.

Daisy shook her head. "They only pay Tanner a quarter of what he was making on the pipeline. He can't make the payments on his new truck nor afford the house he's renting. He hates that I make more money in tips than he does for all the backbreaking work he does all week. He gets so angry." She rubbed her arms, staring past Molly and Kujo as if reliving the past. Then she shook herself and pasted a smile on her face. "I'm sorry. I shouldn't have said all that. Forget it. I broke up with him, anyway. Enjoy your meal." The young woman spun and scurried away.

Molly's heart squeezed in her chest. "That really sucks for her."

"Yeah. When life throws you curve balls. You have to learn how to swing at them." Kujo's gaze followed Daisy to the swinging door to the kitchen.

"Is that what happened to you? Is that why you're working for Hank, now?" Molly stared across the table at the man.

Kujo's lips firmed into a tight line. "The army was all I knew, all I trained for."

"Like Daisy's boyfriend."

He nodded. "When that was no longer an option, I was lost and angry."

"What did you do?"

His lips formed a crooked smile. "I lost myself in the mountains of Colorado."

"Lost yourself?"

"Figuratively speaking. I became a hermit in a cabin in the mountains."

Molly touched his hand. "I'm beginning to see a pattern."

His smile grew softer. "I stayed there for three years, until Bear and Duke came to tell me Six was up for adoption."

Molly studied the strong, vibrant man sitting across from her and marveled at how he had felt lost when he'd left the military. If he could be that angry and disappointed about losing the life he'd come to know, others might feel the same.

"Your friends threw you a lifeline," she said.

He nodded. "That lifeline was Six."

Molly's chest swelled. She'd liked the dog from the first moment they'd met. Now she had even more of a reason to appreciate the animal.

"Six had been injured in his last assignment, and fostering wasn't working out for him. If I hadn't come along, they would have euthanized him."

Molly gasped. "You saved each other."

His lips quirked up on the corners. "I guess we did. Now we have a chance at a new life." Kujo stared at the door to the diner as if he could see Six sitting outside so patiently waiting for them to come out.

Kujo smiled across the table like a man in love.

Molly's heart flipped. What would it be like to have this man's love?

"In the military," he said softly, "we had annual suicide prevention and operations security briefings. In each of the sessions, we were trained to look for signs in our peers and subordinates of depression or extreme stress. Studies showed when things aren't going well at home, either with relationships or financial disasters, good men can be turned bad more easily. They might sell information to the enemy or join the other side to get out of the situation they find themselves in."

"Or commit suicide," Molly added.

"True. The people around here who've lost their jobs are in similar situations. They've become desperate and do stupid things or lash out."

"Like Tanner, Daisy's ex."

He nodded. "I'll bet he isn't the only one who's angry and willing to find an outlet for his anger."

Though they spoke softly, Molly couldn't resist making a casual perusal of the diner to see if anyone was paying attention to them, possibly eavesdropping into their discussion.

Everyone appeared to be concentrating on the people sitting at their own tables, not Molly and Kujo's.

Molly ate the rest of her meal in silence, while listening to the conversations around their table, hoping to glean more information about the layoffs and subsequent relationship issues.

One woman talked about substituting in the local elementary school to a friend who thought it was a good idea. A man complained about the price of feed for his horses to another man who tried to one-up him with the rising cost of fuel for his tractors. None of them appeared to be angry enough to be terrorist recruits.

Except maybe the cranky, bearded man at the counter. Only he didn't look like he was in any condition to run obstacle courses or storm buildings with high-powered machine guns.

Then again, it only took a man driving a vehicle into a crowd to create chaos and fear. Her intel had mentioned an ISIS training camp, not what kind of training they were conducting.

Kujo finished his meal and leaned across the table to grasp her hand. "Penny for your thoughts." He entwined her fingers with his.

Molly's thoughts flew out the window as soon as he touched her. "I wasn't thinking about much," she stalled. "What about you?"

"I was just thinking about how lucky I am to be sitting with the prettiest woman in the diner."

Her cheeks heated, and that kaleidoscope of butterflies took off once again battering her insides with their soft wings. "Be serious," she said, her voice a little breathless.

"I am." He lifted her hand and pressed a kiss to her knuckles. "We have a few minutes before we meet with Mr. Perez. Want to window shop and see what Eagle Rock has to offer?"

Molly practically jumped from her seat, anxious for

any movement that would require Kujo to release her hand.

When he did, she felt the loss immediately and could breathe normally again. Why did this man have such a profound effect on her? "Give me a minute. I want to visit the ladies' room," she said, her heart pounding.

"Take your time."

Molly hurried to the back of the diner where a hallway led to the restrooms. She entered the ladies' room and stood at the sink, staring into the mirror at her flushed face. What was wrong with her? She never reacted to men the way she was reacting to Kujo. If she weren't careful, she'd lose focus on her mission.

Hell, if she weren't careful, she'd fall in love with the former Army soldier.

Molly splashed water on her face, telling herself to snap out of her growing infatuation with the big guy. So, he'd held her hand. He was doing it for their cover. He'd said she was beautiful. Again, for their cover.

She dried her face and straightened. "Now, don't be a fool. Get out there and do your job."

The door to the restroom opened, and Daisy stepped in.

Molly moved aside, but Daisy didn't pass her. Instead, she stopped in front of Molly. "I'm sorry about unloading on you in the diner."

"It's quite all right." Molly touched the young woman's arm. "It's hard breaking up with someone you thought you had a future with."

"I guess it was so new, I couldn't help it. I kicked him

out of my apartment yesterday. I had my apartment manager change the locks while he was away."

Molly gave her a twisted smile. "I bet he wasn't happy when he came back to find that his key didn't work."

"I warned him, but he didn't think I'd do it. I packed all his clothes into bags and set them outside the door. The only thing of his I didn't put out was his laptop. I figure if he wants it enough, he'll have to ask nicely. I put it in the back of my Jeep so I won't have to let him back into the apartment to get it." Daisy looked up, her eyes pooling with tears. "Was I wrong to kick him out? When he hit me, should I have been more understanding?"

Molly's heart hurt for the woman who couldn't be more than twenty-one or twenty-two. She wrapped her arms around Daisy. "Oh, sweetheart, you did the right thing. No man has the right to hit a woman."

"My friend, Martha—her husband hits her all the time. And she just takes it." Daisy shook her head. "Am I weak? Should I stand by my man like Martha does when times are tough?"

"Was her husband laid off like your boyfriend?"

Daisy nodded and swiped at a tear leaking out of the corner of her eye. "They worked together. They still do on the Pinion Ranch. But they're frustrated and not making enough to live on. That's why my boyfriend moved in with me. He couldn't afford an apartment on his own, and now I feel guilty about kicking him out."

"That's his problem. You shouldn't feel guilty. Especially if he's abusing you."

"That's what I keep telling myself. But at the same time, isn't a woman supposed to stand by her man, through good times and bad?" She leaned back and stared into Molly's eyes.

"Not that kind of bad. A guy has to be man enough to handle the bad times without taking it out on the ones he's supposed to love. You're smart. You knew it wasn't right and got out before it got worse. Some women don't figure that out until too late."

Daisy hugged Molly. "I'm so sorry to dump all of this on you. But you seemed so nice, and you aren't related to anyone in Eagle Rock. I knew you'd give me an unbiased opinion."

"Daisy, I'm glad to help. You deserve better, and you're doing the right thing to cut it off before you're hurt badly."

Daisy squeezed her one last time then stepped away, adjusted her apron and wiped the tears from her cheeks. She gave Molly a watery smile. "Thank you."

"If you need me for anything, I'm staying at Mrs. K's B&B. Day or night." Molly took the pad from Daisy's pocket and the pen from behind her ear and wrote her cell phone number on one of the pages. She handed the pad and pen to the woman. "Anytime. I mean it."

Daisy and Molly left the restroom at the same time. Daisy entered the kitchen, while Molly weaved through the tables to where Kujo sat.

He stood as she approached. "Ready to go?"

Kujo paid at the counter, left a tip on the table and called out, "Thank you, Daisy."

Daisy had just walked back through the swinging

kitchen door. She smiled at Kujo and then at Molly. "Thank you."

Molly liked Daisy and hoped her ex-boyfriend didn't try to seek vengeance on the girl.

Before they left the diner, Molly had one thing she wanted to do.

"Hold on," Molly said. She stepped up to the grouchy man at the counter and held out her hand. "Hi, I'm Molly. I thought I'd introduce myself and thank you for your insight on the job situation."

He frowned at the hand held out to him as if it might bite him. Finally, he took it in his meaty palm and practically crushed her fingers.

"And you are?" she asked and smiled brightly through the pain.

"George Batson."

"Mr. Batson, I look forward to running into you again. Thank you for taking time to talk with us about Eagle Rock."

His face turned a ruddy red. "Ain't nothin'. Eagle Rock's a nice place to live, if you have work."

"We think so, too. I hope things improve soon for you and all of those people who lost their jobs."

"Oh, I didn't lose my job. But my sons did, and their friends. Most of them left. The ones still here are making peanuts hauling hay and mucking stalls part time at Pinion Ranch."

"I see." Molly smiled again. "Well, it was a pleasure to meet you." She hooked her arm through Kujo's and left the diner.

"What was that all about?" Kujo asked.

"Your boss, Hank, has connections, right?"

"Yeah. So?"

"Between mine and his, we should feed them names of people we come across who could possibly be involved with terrorists."

Kujo glanced back at George Batson through the windows of the diner. "And you think Batson might be one of them?"

"Maybe. Or his sons." She shrugged. "I'm throwing noodles against the wall, hoping something sticks." She leaned into him, hugging his arm. "Work with me."

Kujo dropped his hand to the small of her back. "Good point. As soon as we get to somewhere private, we can call in the names of the people we just spoke with."

Molly laughed. "You think Daisy might be involved in covert activities?"

"Some say the really bad ones are the folks you least suspect."

Molly nodded. "Well, Daisy would be the least likely candidate in my book. Now, her boyfriend might be someone we consider as well."

"Names, sweetheart," Kujo said. "We need first and last names."

"I didn't get Tanner's last name." Molly had been so wrapped up in Daisy's story, she'd forgotten to ask for the name of her boyfriend. Then she relaxed. "I know someone who can help."

"Who?"

"Mrs. K at the B&B. She said she's been in Eagle

Rock all her life. She's proud of the fact she knows everyone."

Kujo grinned. "A busybody."

"Of the best kind," Molly agreed.

"What about Perez?" Kujo asked. "Should we add him to the list of potential suspects?"

"Wouldn't hurt to run his name through some criminal databases to see if we come up with a match." She held up her cell phone. "I even snapped a photo of him while his attention was on George."

Kujo leaned back, his eyes wide. "Damn, woman, you really are in it to win it."

"You bet I am. I have a lot riding on this investigation," she whispered, the smile dropping from her lips. "This is my first field assignment. If I screw it up, I'm back at a desk." She sighed. "I hate paperwork."

CHAPTER 12

THEY WALKED to the end of Main Street and a little farther, out of range of the houses and any nosey neighbors. At the end of town, Molly called her supervisor, Pete, gave him Batson and Perez's names and asked him to scan the criminal data bases for any hits.

While Molly talked to her boss, Kujo placed a call to Hank, giving him the same information. When they ended their calls, they turned and headed back into Eagle Rock. They were halfway back to the diner when they saw Perez enter one of the buildings. It appeared to be the one they'd passed with pictures of houses posted on the insides of the windows.

"Give him another fifteen minutes to set up appointments, then we'll step in. In the meantime, let's go in here," Molly steered Kujo into the first store they came to. Six sat outside the door and waited patiently.

It just so happened the store was filled with baby and maternity items.

"Oops." Molly fought the smile threatening to spill across her face. "Guess I should have looked first."

"Hello. Welcome to First Comes Love." A petite and very pregnant woman waddled toward them. "Can I help you find anything?"

Molly shot a glance at Kujo and nearly burst out laughing. "We're just browsing right now."

"Oh, please. Take your time," the young lady said. "When are you expecting?"

Molly laid a hand over her flat belly. "Not for a while," she said, choking down a giggle.

"I'm Simone. If you have questions, feel free to ask." She rubbed a hand over her belly. "Don't worry. This isn't my first baby; I have three more with the sitter. I can tell you just about anything you might want to know about having babies."

"Thank you. I'll keep that in mind." Molly dragged Kujo deeper into the store. "What do you think about this crib?" Molly stopped by one painted white. "Or do you prefer the darker one?"

"I actually hadn't thought about either." Kujo tugged at the collar of his T-shirt, a fine sheen of sweat breaking out on his forehead. "Isn't it a little soon to be looking at cribs?"

"It's never too soon. You'd be surprised at all of the furniture and equipment available to make your baby more comfortable." Simone appeared beside them. "Do you know if it's a boy or a girl, yet?"

Kujo coughed. "Absolutely not."

"Oh, are you going to be surprised, then?" Simone smiled. "I was surprised with my second one. They told me it was a girl, but his little thingy was hiding every time we did the ultrasound." Simone made a motion with her finger, indicating the baby's penis. "We welcomed him into a pink baby room. Oh, my husband painted it within a week, but we're very happy to have our little Robbie. He's three now."

"Uh. I think I need some air," Kujo bolted for the door.

Simone stared after him. "Is he going to be all right?"

Molly laughed out loud. "I don't think he's quite ready for all of this."

Simone smiled. "Are they ever? My husband always turns a little pale when I tell him I'm pregnant again. I'm just thankful he has a good job with the sheriff's department, what with so many people out of work lately. But he loves every one of our babies, and he's a good father."

If she weren't on a mission, Molly would have spent more time with the woman. "I'd better catch up with my fiancé before he runs clear to the next county. Thank you for your assistance." She hurried out of the store, chuckling all the way. When she caught up with Kujo and Six outside, she couldn't wipe the grin off her face. "I'm sorry." She touched his arm. "That was unfair of me."

"I was good up to..." He crooked his finger like Simone had.

Molly grinned. "I liked Simone. She's very passionate about her job."

"That's not the only thing she's passionate about. Three kids and another on the way?" He shook his head.

Molly fell in step beside him. "How many children is the right number?"

"I don't know...2.5?" He shoved a hand through his hair.

Molly almost felt sorry for him. But not quite. "I always pictured having four children like Simone. I grew up an only child. I wouldn't wish that on any kid."

"I'm one of five. I'm not sure I'd wish that on any kid."

"Did you like your siblings?"

"For the most part. My mother didn't see fit to give us a sister to tone us down, so we fought, wrestled and broke things."

"And I bet you'd fight to your last breath for any one of them."

Kujo didn't say anything for a moment. "Yeah. I'd give my life for them."

"How long has it been since you've visited your siblings?"

He shrugged. "Four or five years."

She stared at him with a frown puckering her brows. "Are you kidding me? If I had siblings, I'd make it a point to visit them more often."

"We all went our separate ways after high school. I went into the Army, two of my brothers joined the Marines. Another went to college and is an engineer working for one of the big aircraft manufacturers. The other stayed on the ranch down in Texas to work the horses and cattle my father raises."

"And you haven't been back to Texas?"

Kujo shook his head.

"Why?"

He turned away and stared up at the mountains. "It doesn't matter."

"It must or you'd have gone back to visit. Do you and your parents get along?"

"Sure. It's not like that."

"It's about losing yourself in the mountains, isn't it?"

"Yeah. Pretty much."

"I'm glad you found yourself." Molly wanted to wipe the grim look off his face. "And it's a good thing. If we're having children together, I insist on them knowing their grandparents."

He whipped his head around to stare at her in alarm.

She grinned and hooked her arm through his. "Don't sweat it. I guess I'm jealous of your family and wanted to live vicariously. I'm sure your reasons are good." She leaned her head against his shoulder. "We should go look at property. I hope we find what we're looking for."

DAVID PEREZ MET them at the door. He had a list of properties to show them and had called ahead to warn the sellers they would be coming.

"Do I need to take my dog back to the B&B?" Kujo asked.

David glanced down at Six. "Is he friendly?"

"He's well-behaved," Kujo said.

Perez seemed to think about it then shrugged. "He can ride in the back."

They loaded into Perez's SUV and set off on the hunt for property.

After the first three places proved to be small acreages, not nearly close enough to the area Molly had hoped to explore, she took the matter into her own hands. "I was really hoping to get closer to the mountains. Is there any property for sale in that direction?" She pointed to the hills she'd gone into two days before. "All of what you've shown us is too small. Think bigger. And we don't mind remote."

David's brows dipped. "Have you ever been in Montana during the winter? Remote can be the difference between accessible and cut off."

"We're from Wisconsin," Molly said, coming up with the first cold state she could think of. "We know how to deal with snow."

"Wisconsin doesn't have the mountains Montana does."

"Like I said, my fiancée is an avid photographer," Kujo said. "She wants to live as close to nature as she can. Her photographs can be seen in all of the nature magazines."

"Could you drive that way and tell us a little about the larger tracts of land?" Molly asked. "Who owns them? Are they friendly? Would they mind an outsider moving in next door?"

Perez turned the SUV around and drove in the direction Molly had pointed. "I haven't called any of the property owners," he said.

"Can we drive up into some of the hills and find a vantage point where we can look out over the area from higher up?" Kujo asked.

Molly clapped her hands. "Great idea. That might

give us a better understanding of the terrain and available properties."

"There isn't any place like that."

"No?" Molly blinked up at the realtor, giving him her most innocent look.

"Most views are blocked by tall trees." Perez shook his head. "I'd take you up into the mountains, but it'll be dark soon, and I wouldn't want to get us lost finding our way back out."

"Understandable," Kujo agreed. "Maybe tomorrow."

Molly recognized the dirt road she'd turned off on the day she'd gone out on the four-wheeler. "I adore this area. The trees are so tall and lush. Is this property for sale?"

Perez snorted. "Not hardly. It's a three-thousand-acre ranch owned by Paul Tilson."

"Oh, my." She pushed out her bottom lip in a pout. "I know we can't afford that much land, but do you think we could ask him to sell off a small corner?"

"No," Perez said, his tone unbending. Final.

Molly studied Perez.

His face was firm, unyielding. She found it intriguing. Perhaps he'd asked Tilson on previous occasions and been rebuffed.

Still, she persisted. "Can't we even ask?"

"He rarely visits the Pinion Ranch, and he's even harder to get in touch with. He contracted me with the authority to hire people to maintain the house and fences, but asked not to be troubled otherwise."

Molly frowned. "That's strange. With such a pretty place you'd think he'd be here all the time."

"Well, he isn't," Perez said, his voice curt.

"What about on the south side of his place? Is there anything available?" Kujo asked.

"No, that property is part of the National Forest."

PEREZ STEPPED ON THE ACCELERATOR, skimming past the rest of the countryside, headed back into town. "Drop you off somewhere?"

"At the diner would be fine. We can walk from there, thank you," Molly said.

"I'll look at the MLS system and see if I can come up with anything else for tomorrow."

"Have you always lived in Eagle Rock?" Kujo asked. "I wondered, because you know so much about the town and the surrounding countryside.

"My parents moved here when I was just shy of my fourteenth birthday. I've been here ever since."

"And your parents?" Molly asked.

"They moved on to California."

Molly tilted her head. "I imagine real estate gets you around."

"True. I know just about every property in this county and many of the surrounding counties."

The sun was on its way toward the horizon as they neared town.

Red and blue lights flashed as emergency vehicles crowded the streets. Molly leaned forward and peered through the windshield. "What's going on at the diner?"

"I was wondering that myself." Perez parked several blocks away. "This is as close as I can get."

"That's fine," Kujo said. "We can walk." He leaped out and let Six out of the back.

Molly glanced across at Perez. "Thanks for your assistance. We'll be in touch when we're ready to look some more."

Perez had turned away and had his cell phone pressed to his ear as he hurried toward his office.

Kujo and Six joined Molly. "Ready?"

She nodded. "Let's go."

As they neared the emergency vehicles, a sheriff's deputy stepped in front of them. "I'm sorry, but you'll have to take another road through town. They're conducting a crime scene investigation."

"What crime?"

"Someone set off an explosion at the diner. Several people were injured."

Molly's pulse quickened. "An explosion? Was Daisy, the waitress, one of the injured people?"

The deputy held up his hands. "That's all I know. The EMTs are working it, and the state police crime lab is on its way."

Kujo cupped Molly's arm and guided her down a street to one block over that ran parallel to Main Street. They reached the B&B a couple minutes later.

Mrs. K was in the dining area sitting beside a police scanner. When she saw them walk in the door, she leaped to her feet and hurried toward them. "I was worried about you two. Someone blew up the diner."

"We heard." Molly hugged the older woman. "Any news on who was hurt in the explosion?"

"I've only heard the names of a few. Al was knocked

163

off his feet in the kitchen. He might have a concussion. And Daisy Bishop was taken to the trauma center in Bozeman."

"Any idea why the diner was targeted?" Molly asked.

"Someone saw Tanner Birge running from the scene." Mrs. K's eyes rounded. "The sheriff has a BOLO out for him. I knew that boy wasn't good enough for our Daisy."

"Daisy's ex-boyfriend?" Kujo asked.

Mrs. K nodded.

Molly's fists tightened. *The bastard.* "He's mad because she dumped him."

Mrs. K's brows rose. "She did?"

Molly nodded.

"About damned time. He didn't treat her right."

The police scanner crackled.

"I better go and listen." Mrs. K spun and ran across the dining room to where she'd been sitting when they'd entered.

Molly was already halfway to the stairs when Kujo and Six caught up to her.

"Are you thinking what I'm thinking?"

She shot a glance back at him. "Probably. Where would a country boy learn how to set explosives?"

Kujo's lips firmed into a straight line. "At the local terrorist training camp."

CHAPTER 13

AS SOON AS Kujo entered the room he shared with Molly, he pulled his cell phone from his pocket. Just as he was about to hit Hank's number, the phone rang. Hank's name came up on the viewing screen.

Kujo answered. "Hank."

"I guess you've heard."

"About the explosion?" Kujo asked.

"Yeah. I'm listening on the police scanner. They've cornered a guy named Tanner Birge."

Kujo gripped the phone tighter. "Wow. He's the ex-boyfriend of Daisy Bishop, a waitress at Al's Diner."

"The sheriff's department says the explosion wasn't the typical Molotov cocktail or fertilizer, home-made job."

"Are you thinking he had some training?"

"It's possible," Hank said. "I'll see what I can do to get a ring-side seat at the interrogation when they bring him in." Hank paused. Voices and the staticky noise of a radio sounded in the background. "Hold on, Kujo. We're getting more information."

Molly stood beside Kujo and tilted her head close to his hand holding the cell phone. "What's going on?"

"They've cornered Tanner Birge," he whispered.

She nodded and leaned closer, her hair brushing across his skin. The peachy scent of her shampoo invaded his senses.

"What a cluster-fuck," Hank said when he came back on the line.

"What's happening?"

"He was headed north toward Canada, when they forced his truck off the road. He had his hands up, getting out of the vehicle, when some trigger-happy son-of-a-bitch fired a shot. In the confusion, Birge got away."

"Who fired the shot?" Molly asked.

"They don't know. They're checking everyone's weapons. Wait..." More voices and static sounded through the receiver.

Kujo tapped the phone, engaging the speaker option, and held it between himself and Molly.

She captured his gaze and held it.

"Are you still there?" Hank asked.

"We're here," Kujo responded.

"It appears none of the deputies discharged their weapons."

Molly shook her head. "How can that be?" As soon as the words were out of her mouth her eyes rounded.

Kujo's jaw tightened. "Sniper."

"I'm running Birge's name through my people," Hank said.

Molly tipped her head over the phone and spoke, "I'll contact my supervisor and get the folks back in the office working it, too."

"Someone didn't want Birge talking about where he got those explosives," Kujo stated.

"Do you think his ex-girlfriend could be in trouble, too?" Molly asked.

"If anyone thinks she has information about who Birge hung out with, she might be the next target," Kujo added.

"Taz is back from assignment. I'll put him on her. He can provide the protection she might need, and also question her when she's able to answer. Whatever he finds out, I'll pass on to you."

"Good."

"In the meantime," Hank continued, "hang tight until we know something."

Kujo nodded. "Will do."

"Out, here," Hank said.

"Out, here." Kujo ended the call and lowered the phone. "We need to know as much about Tanner Birge as we can find out." He paced to the end of the room and back. "Who are his friends? Where do they hang out, and what he might have stored in his apartment?"

Molly shook her head. "I can't believe he moved on Daisy so quickly. Poor Daisy." She stared across the floor at Kujo. "I bet he was so mad he nearly hit the roof when he found his stuff outside her apartment and the door locks changed." Her eyes widened and a grin spread across her face. "I know where we might get some information on him."

"Yeah? Where?"

"His laptop."

"I'm sure the sheriff's deputies and crime scene investigators have confiscated his laptop by now, since he had all his belongings in his truck."

Molly's grin widened. "Not all of his things were in his truck. His laptop is in Daisy's Jeep." Molly strode to the closet, pulled out a long-sleeved black turtleneck shirt and tossed it on the bed.

"Why would it be in her car?"

"She didn't want him to have a reason to enter her apartment again. She was going to give it to him one day when he was in town and being reasonable." Molly pulled her shirt up over her head and tossed it beside the black one.

Kujo's heart flipped, and his groin tightened. He stood like a statue, all the blood in his head, rushing to his dick. "Uh..." he cleared his throat, "Don't you think we should go get the laptop?"

She laughed. "That's what I'm doing. Don't you have dark clothing you can wear? It's dark out, now. We don't want anyone to see us, do we?"

Kujo's cheeks heated, and he pulled his brain out of his pants. "Right." He dug in his duffel bag for a long-sleeved black T-shirt he'd purchased at the feed store and stripped out of the blue chambray shirt he'd worn all day.

When he glanced across at Molly, she stood with her

lips parted, her gaze traveling over his chest and downward to the waistband of his jeans.

"Like what you see?" he joked, his smile fading as he studied her in her bra and jeans. "Because I sure as hell like what I see."

He closed the distance between them and took her hands in his. "We could wait for it to get darker, and for the streets to empty before we hunt for Birge's laptop." He raised her hands and laid them on his chest. "You're not resisting. I'll take that as a good sign you won't coldcock me for doing this." He bent and brushed his lips across hers.

Molly pressed her hands to his chest, her fingers curling into his skin, her nails digging into the flesh.

Sweet Jesus, he couldn't let go of her. The laptop would wait while Kujo drank his fill of the beautiful FBI agent.

He slipped his hands down her naked back, careful of her cuts and bruises, stopping at the stiff cotton of her denim jeans.

Molly lowered one of her hands to his and guided his fingers beneath the waistband of her pants and panties.

Kujo's cock strained against the confines of his zipper. He wanted to toss Molly over his shoulder and carry her to the bed where he'd plunge deep inside her.

Instead, he skimmed the line of her lips until she opened to him on a sigh.

Go slowly. A woman didn't want a man pawing her. Besides, he wanted her as hot and ready for him as he was for her.

He thrust his tongue between her teeth and caressed her in a warm, wet slide. With his hands, he cupped her ass and kneaded the flesh, loving how her muscles flexed and released.

She wrapped her calf around the back of his leg, and pulled herself closer until her sex rubbed against his thigh, with only the layers of denim in the way.

Molly slipped her hand between them, flicked the button on his jeans and eased the zipper down.

Immediately, his cock sprang free, nudging the backs of her knuckles.

She captured him in her grip, holding him firmly, her slim hands making him even harder than steel.

Molly looked up into his eyes. "I don't need foreplay this time. I want you now. Inside me, don't pass GO, don't think you have to get me there. Trust me...I'm so hot, I think I'll spontaneously combust if we don't do it now."

"Damn, Molly. If you're not ready..."

"What did I just say?" She pushed his jeans over his hips and down his legs.

He toed off his boots and stepped out of them and his pants.

She stared at him, her gaze traveling from his chest down his abs to stop at his jutting erection. Her eyes flared, and her tongue swept across her bottom lip. "What are you waiting for?"

"First things first." Kujo lunged for his wallet in the back pocket of his jeans, scrounged for the condom packet he always kept there and held it up, relief flooding through him. He tossed it on the nightstand.

Then he scooped her in his arms, fused her lips with his in a scorching kiss and then laid her on the mattress.

He pulled her legs over the edge of the bed, stripped off her jeans and panties, parted her thighs and stepped between them. "I'll show you romance." He bent over her, nudging her entrance with his cock. But he wasn't going for the gold yet. Despite her words to the contrary, he wanted her to orgasm before him.

Kujo reached behind her, unclipped her bra and slid the straps from her shoulders. He cupped her breasts in his palms and gently squeezed them. Then he captured one perky nubbin with his lips. Sucking gently, he pulled it into his mouth, tongued the nipple and rolled it between his teeth.

She arched her back off the mattress. "I want you, now," she moaned.

He rolled his face to the side and gasped. "Patience, I'm not ready."

"The hell you aren't. I saw the evidence," she protested. "Please..."

Ignoring her entreaty, he moved his mouth to claim the other breast, flicking her nipple with his tongue and rolling the tip between his teeth. When she was squirming beneath him, he moved down her torso, tonguing and kissing a gentle path over each rib to her bellybutton and lower to the tuft of hair covering her sex.

She weaved her fingers into his hair and urged him even lower. "Now that you've started along this path...*finish*." She widened her legs.

Kujo traced a finger down her center, over her clit to

her damp entrance, where he swirled in her juices. A large, work-roughened finger poked inside her, then another and another, until he stretched her opening and pushed inside.

Molly moaned, her bottom twisting against the comforter, her fingers tightening their hold on his hair.

Kujo parted her folds with his thumbs and blew a stream of air across her nubbin.

"Oh, sweet heaven, do me already," she cried.

Kujo chuckled. "As you wish." He flicked his tongue against her clitoris.

Molly's back rose off the bed, and her fingernails dug into his scalp. "Again!" she begged.

He obliged. This time he dragged his tongue across that strip of nerve-packed flesh, swirled and ended on a flick.

Molly lifted her knees. "Joe, this is absolute torture."

He lifted his head. "Do you want me to stop?"

"Hell, no!"

Knowing he had her where he wanted her, he bent to the task of taking her over the top by tonguing, nibbling and sucking on her until she bucked beneath him, her body stiffening to the point she stopped breathing altogether. She raised her hips even closer to his mouth, her body trembling with her orgasm.

Kujo didn't stop until Molly lowered her bottom to the bed and tugged his hair.

He moved upward, repeating his downward journey in the opposite direction, kissing her torso, nibbling her nipples and finally claiming her lips.

Molly wrapped toned legs around his waist and locked her heels behind him.

He slipped an arm beneath her back, lifted her up onto the bed and lay down between her legs. "Say no now and I'll back away."

She lifted her head. "Are you kidding me?"

He laughed. "I didn't say it would be easy, but I wanted to give you the chance to stop."

"Don't be a tease. I want it all." She tightened her legs around him and pulled herself up to where his cock pressed against her pussy.

"Okay, okay." He unwrapped her legs from around him and pressed her head against the pillow with a long, soul-defining kiss. He leaned away from her, grabbed the foil packet and tore it open.

Impatient fingers took the condom from him and slipped it over his cock. At the base, she paused long enough to fondle his balls, squeezed him, and then guided him to her entrance. "Now, don't tease me anymore." She swirled the tip of his dick in her moisture. "I'm ready for whatever you've got. The harder and faster, the better."

With permission granted, Kujo let loose, driving into her like a sword into its scabbard—hard, deep and sure. He didn't stop until he was buried to the hilt, his balls slapping her buttocks. Once inside, he stopped, allowing her to adjust to his thickness and to allow him to remember how to breathe.

Then he settled into a slow, steady rhythm, pulling out, thrusting in, coating his shaft in her juices and enjoying the tightness of her grip on him.

She dropped her feet to the mattress. Each time he pulled out, she rose, digging her heels into the mattress, following him. When he pressed back inside, she met him at the end of each thrust.

His tension increased and, with it, his speed, until he hammered in and out of her, moving faster and faster.

Molly sank her fingers into his ass, clutching him, guiding him to slam even harder until he rocketed to the edge and over, his orgasm sending him into the stratosphere. He dropped down on her, holding himself just above her, his cock buried deep, his breathing as ragged as a marathon runner's pushing through to the finish.

He could have stayed there forever, but if he lowered himself more, his weight would crush the air from her lungs and add pain to her already bruised ribs. Kujo rolled to his side, taking her with him. He lay there for a long time, strumming his fingers from the swell of her breasts, down the curve of her waist to the flare of her hips and back.

Molly lay back against the pillow and raised an arm over her head. "Wow."

"Agreed," Kujo said. "If I had it in me, I'd say let's do that again. Now."

"I've never felt anything as intense," she whispered into the air. "Ever."

"Nor have I," he said, and meant it. None of the women he'd slept with in the past had brought him that close to heaven before "We have to do that again."

Molly nodded. "Damn right." She lay for a long time, one hand tangled in his hair.

The last thing Kujo wanted to do was leave the bed, but duty called. He leaned up on his elbow and stared down into her eyes. "Well?"

She nodded. "It's that time, isn't it?"

He nodded. "Let's go find a laptop." He kissed her hard, thrusting his tongue into her mouth.

She wrapped her arm around his neck and kissed him back, coming up for air at the same time.

His cock thickened, but he couldn't put off what they had to do any longer, and he didn't have another condom. He rolled to the edge of the bed, disposed of the condom and pushed to his feet. Grabbing his jeans, he jammed his legs into them, before he changed his mind and made love to Molly again.

She rolled out of the bed and stood before him naked, more beautiful than he could have imagined, her auburn hair cascading around her shoulders in a shiny mass.

He gripped her arms and gazed into her eyes. "This isn't over by a long shot. You know that, right?"

She grinned up at him. "I certainly hope not. If we didn't have a job to do, I'd have gone for another round."

Kujo laughed, feeling lighter and happier than he had in what seemed like forever. He slapped her bare bottom and squeezed it. "Get dressed, or I might throw you back on the bed before we get out the door."

She found her jeans across the room and slipped her legs into them. "Promises, promises."

He couldn't stop looking as she put on her bra and the black turtleneck shirt.

Kujo dressed in dark clothing and found the dark

knit hat he'd purchased in the store, pulling it down over his ears.

When he faced Molly, he was amazed at the transformation. From naked siren to sexy alley cat, she was as stunning in her stealth clothes as she was without. He pulled her into his arms and kissed her again. "Ready?"

Molly smirked. "For what? To strip naked and climb back in the bed with you?" She nodded. "To go sneak into a woman's car for a laptop that might point to the leader of the ISIS training effort in the area?" She shrugged. "Sure. Let's do this." She glanced down at Six. "What about our friend?"

Kujo gazed at the animal that had lain quietly in a corner during their sexual encounter. The dog had manners. "He can come. He's dark enough he won't be easily seen in the shadows. But first, we need to locate Daisy's Jeep."

"IT'S PROBABLY at the diner since she was at work when the explosion happened." Molly reached for his hand and held it in hers. "Or it could still be parked at her apartment, depending on how close it is to her job."

Kujo liked that she'd reached for his hand and reveled in the warmth of hers. He wanted more of her than just her hand. He wanted her mind, her body and her heart.

Oh, hell, where was he going with this infatuation? They barely knew each other. He had to stay focused on the task at hand. He could sort through his feelings after they found the source of the terrorist training effort. "Any idea where Daisy lives?"

"No, but I bet I know someone who does." She led him downstairs to the dining room where Mrs. K was listening intently to the conversations going on with the police band radio.

"Mrs. K, I'd like to run by Daisy's apartment building and let the manager know what's going on with Daisy. Do you know where she lives?"

Mrs. K jumped up and turned down the scanner. "She lives in the apartment building two blocks south of the diner." The B&B owner's brows furrowed. "Is there anything I can do to help?"

"Pray." Molly said and hurried out the door, dragging Kujo behind her and with Six bringing up the rear.

Once outside, Molly paused.

"Walk or drive?" Kujo asked.

"Walk. If anyone else has the same idea and knows where that laptop is, we could have some competition."

CHAPTER 14

MOLLY CHOSE to remain in the shadows as they passed from house to house via back alleys to within view of the diner. If someone else was after the laptop, she wanted to see them, not the other way around. If they managed to get to the laptop first, she didn't want anyone tracing it back to her and Kujo. That would put them at risk until they learned whether or not there was any information worth hacking off the machine.

The fire department had long since rolled up their hoses and driven away. A sheriff's deputy's patrol car stood guard on the street in front of the diner. The state crime lab would be there the next day to sift through the rubble to determine the source of the explosion, even though the fire chief had given his findings. The state crime lab folks might be able to trace the parts and pieces back to the source. Molly doubted it.

"I don't see a Jeep. Daisy said she put his laptop in her Jeep."

"If it suffered any damage, the sheriff could have had it towed to an impound lot."

"In this small of a town?" Molly shook her head. "I would think everything would have to remain in place until the crime lab arrives. Let's check her apartment."

They slipped away, traveling through a back alley the two blocks away from the diner to the apartment complex Mrs. K had indicated. In the parking lot was an older-model Jeep with a daisy flower decal on the back windshield.

Kujo chuckled. "Could she have made it easier to identify?"

Six sat at Kujo's feet, looking up at him, waiting for a command.

They stood near bushes. The moon shone down from overhead, casting a bright glow over the parking lot and Daisy's Jeep. They'd have to step out into the open to reach the vehicle.

"I'll go." Molly pulled her stocking cap down over her face and tucked her hair beneath it.

"No, I should go," Kujo insisted.

"Is your gun loaded?" Molly asked.

"Yes, of course, it is."

"Then stay here and provide cover."

He shook his head. "I should go, and you should provide cover."

"Six responds to you. If you go, he might follow."

"Six will do as I tell him." Kujo's jaw firmed in the limited lighting.

"Look, this is my job. Let me do it."

"I don't know where in the FBI training manual it

says breaking into a vehicle is part of your job description."

She pulled what appeared to be a long flat file out of her sleeve and held it up. "I won't be breaking anything. But I know how to use it, and you don't." Molly grinned. "Now, stay with Six while I do what we came here for."

Kujo didn't appear to like it, but he stood stoically in the shadows and drew his weapon from the holster beneath his jacket. "Okay, but don't be long. If you don't get it open on the first couple of tries, come back."

"I'll get in," she promised.

Just as Molly was about to step out of the shadows into the light, a hand caught her arm and yanked her back hard against a wall of muscles.

"What the—" she started.

Kujo's hand clamped over her mouth, and he whispered in her ear. "Shh. Watch." He dropped his hand from her mouth and motioned to the dog.

Molly held perfectly still and scanned the parking lot and apartment building. A movement alerted her to the fact they were not alone.

A dark figure detached itself from the shrubbery on the far end of the lot and hurried toward the apartment building and up the stairs to one of the doors. A light shined down on the figure. Like Molly and Kujo, the figure was covered in dark clothing, with the addition of a ski mask. He tried the door, but it wouldn't open. Then he cocked his leg and kicked the door. The sound echoed against the walls of the other units, but no one came out to investigate.

Again, the burglar kicked the door. The sharp crack

of wood splitting could be heard all the way out to where Molly and Kujo hunkered in the shadows.

"We have to get to the Jeep before he discovers the laptop isn't in the apartment," Molly whispered.

The intruder disappeared into Daisy's unit.

"What if he has a sidekick covering his back?" Kujo asked.

Molly shook her head. "It's a risk we have to take. "I'll stay low and use the Jeep for cover." She didn't wait for his response. Molly ducked low and ran for the Jeep. She didn't slow until she reached the passenger door, where she paused to catch her breath and will her pulse to slow.

When she had her heart rate under control, she raised her hand, slipped the flat file between the window and the door and slid it down inside the panel. Moving it closer to the door lock, she raised it slowly, searching for the mechanism. She engaged nothing but air. Pushing the file back down, she moved it over a little and tried again. As she pulled it up, she glanced toward Daisy's apartment door.

The file engaged with metal. As she dragged it upward, the lock disengaged. Her heartbeat speeding, she glanced up again to reassure herself no one was coming down the stairs.

Then she lifted the handle on the door and opened it. As soon as she did, the overhead light blinked on.

Damn. She'd forgotten about the automatic lights. Too late, she didn't have time to find the switch to turn it off. Molly checked the front seat and floorboard, without finding a computer or case.

She hit the lock mechanism, unlocking all the doors and closed the front door softly. The overhead light blinked out. Molly glanced at the apartment. Again, no one had emerged. Moving to the back door, she eased it open. Again, the light clicked on.

There, on the back floorboard was a black case the size that would fit a laptop. She lifted it. It was heavy enough to be a laptop. Taking the time to check, she looked over the top of the back seat into the back of the vehicle. It was empty, as was the rest of the back seat.

Molly slipped out of the vehicle and carefully closed the door. The light blinked out. A movement out of the corner of her eye caught her attention. Someone emerged from Daisy's apartment and ran down the stairs.

Sure the intruder hadn't spotted her in the moon shadow of the Jeep, Molly lay flat and rolled beneath the vehicle, clutching the laptop to her chest. She lay still, holding her breath. Footsteps sounded across the gravel and stopped beside her, within two feet of where she lay.

She prayed Kujo didn't get trigger-happy and start shooting. If the person were looking for the laptop in Daisy's Jeep, he'd have easy access with the doors unlocked. He wouldn't find anything inside, and he would go away, none the wiser of the woman who hid beneath the chassis.

The moon had risen higher in the sky, beaming down on the gravel parking lot. It glinted off something shiny near to where Molly hid.

Damn! Her heart stopped and shuddered, and then

beat a thousand beats a second. The file she'd used to trigger the lock lay within inches of her face. If the intruder bothered to look down, he'd see it. If he bent to pick it up, he'd see her lying beneath the vehicle.

A vehicle drove by the apartment building. The man turned toward it, his feet pointing away from the Jeep and the file.

Molly reached out, grabbed the file and pulled it to her chest. The file bumped against the under carriage making a clanking sound. Molly froze.

The feet spun toward her again.

A light shone into the parking lot. Her intruder ducked down low enough, Molly could see his knees. She closed her eyelids to keep him from seeing the whites of her eyes and waited for the next move. A scuffle of gravel indicated someone was moving away.

Molly opened her eyes and watched the intruder running for the bushes close to where Kujo and Six waited for her.

Holy hell. Molly slid the laptop and file off her chest, pulled the H&K pistol from the holster beneath her jacket and aimed at the man's back. If he tried to hurt Kujo or Six, she'd take him down without hesitation.

The bushes parted, and the man disappeared.

A woman and a man got out of a car nearby, talking about their visit to his mother's house and plans for the following day. They entered one of the ground-floor apartments, and the world returned to silence.

Molly lay for a long moment, waiting for the reassuring sound of crickets chirping.

When she was certain no one else was moving

about, she started to roll from beneath the Jeep only to find a nose poking beneath the side, sniffing.

Six.

Behind him, Kujo squatted beside the vehicle. "Are you all right?" he asked.

"I'm fine. Are you?" Molly handed him the file and the case with the laptop, and rolled clear of the Jeep. "I was afraid you'd shoot that man," Molly said, her voice shaking slightly.

"I almost did. I was afraid he was going to shoot you. He had a gun in his hand."

Molly shook her head. "I couldn't see that, or I might have shot him when he ran toward you."

Kujo pulled her into his arms. "We're a pair. It's a good thing we didn't pull the triggers."

She leaned into him for a moment, enjoying his strength and outdoorsy scent. Finally, she pulled away. "We have to see what's in this."

"You know we're tampering with evidence, don't you?"

"Yes, but if we get in and figure out what's on there, we can get it back into her car before anyone knows it was ever missing."

"Let's get it to Hank." Kujo grinned. "He's got people."

"We can also get Daisy's permission to enter her vehicle, if she's conscious. After being blown up, I'm positive she'll give it." Molly led the way back to the B&B where Kujo had parked his truck earlier that day.

Six jumped into the back seat.

Kujo drove, and Molly sat back in the passenger seat,

thinking through all that had happened in less than twenty-four hours and all that could happen in the next twenty-four.

Hopefully, the laptop would give them the information they needed to locate the ringleader of the ISIS training camp.

KUJO PHONED Hank as soon as he got into the truck, giving him the heads-up about the apartment break-in and the computer they'd confiscated. "We'll need a computer guru, ASAP."

"Got it," Hank said. "And I'll let the sheriff know about the break-in."

"Good," Kujo said. "Have you heard from Taz? Is Daisy conscious?"

"I have, and she was. She's given her statement to the sheriff, but it won't help. She didn't see anything. Al, the owner, is in critical condition. He suffered a heart attack along with the injuries due to the explosion."

Kujo's lips pressed together. "Text Taz's number to me. We need to talk to Daisy."

"Texting now."

"Thanks." Kujo ended the call as a ping sounded on his cell phone. He slowed near the edge of town and pulled to the side of the road to read the message.

"What's going on?" Molly asked.

"Daisy's awake."

"Do we need to drive to Bozeman to interview her?"

"I think Taz can handle it." He placed the call.

Taz answered on the first ring. "Yeah."

"This is Kujo, one of Hank's new guys."

"Oh, hi. Welcome to the team. What can I do for you?"

"Is Daisy awake?" he asked. "I need to ask her some questions."

"The sheriff's been in and questioned her, but she didn't see anything."

"I know. I have some different questions to ask her."

"I'll check." Taz paused. A few moments later, he came back online. "She's awake. I have you on speaker."

Kujo handed the phone to Molly.

"Hi, Daisy, it's Molly from this morning. How are you feeling?" Molly asked.

"I've been better," she said, her voice sounding small. "The doctor says I can go home tomorrow."

"You might want to stay with family until you're back to one-hundred percent," Molly warned her.

"I will," Daisy agreed.

"Daisy, I work with the FBI."

"Seriously? You're being here...was it a coincidence?"

"No, Daisy. I've been conducting an investigation. I'm really sorry you got caught up in all of this. I had no idea where my investigation was leading."

"It's not your fault. My ex..." she paused to take a deep breath, "what he did... I still can't believe it. My poor boss..." She cleared her throat. "How can I help?"

"Daisy, you said you had Tanner's computer in your Jeep. We think we might get information off of it that can help us find any others who might have helped him with the explosives. Will you give me permission to get that computer out of your vehicle?"

"Sure. Help yourself. From what they told me, Tanner's on the run from the law. He won't be using it." Daisy's voice shook as she finished the statement.

"I'm sorry about what happened with Tanner." Molly said. "I'm sure it must hurt."

"I shouldn't be sad. The man tried to kill me." Daisy sniffed and began to cry. "And to think, I would have married him, if everything hadn't gone to hell."

"I understand." Molly waited for the sobs to slow. "Daisy, one other thing. Do you know the password for Tanner's computer?"

"I don't...wait...I think it's my birthday." She gave Molly the month, day and year. "If you need anything else, just ask. I hate to think someone else helped him. Al's in the ICU, and they say he might not make it."

"I'll keep Al in my prayers. Now you worry about getting well. We'll let you know what we find, if we do find anything." Molly handed the phone to Kujo.

"Hi, Daisy. Let me speak with Taz." He waited a moment and then asked, "Taz, everything going okay there?"

"All's well. I won't let anyone get past me to Daisy."

Kujo ended the call and put the truck in motion. Minutes later, they pulled up to Hank's house on the ranch.

Hank stepped out on the porch, wearing a T-shirt and sweats. "Swede's my tech guru. He's on his way. He and Allie were at the Blue Moose Tavern when I called.

They should be here momentarily." He grinned and nodded his head toward the drive.

Kujo turned to see lights coming toward them.

"That will be them."

A truck pulled up beside Kujo's, and the tall blond man Kujo had met before stepped out and rounded to help an auburn-haired woman down, but she'd beat him to it and let herself out, dropping to the ground. She took Swede's hand and joined Hank, Kujo and Molly.

"Hi, I'm Allie, Hanks's sister." She smiled and held out her hand.

Molly shook her hand. "Nice to meet you. I'm Molly."

"Joe Kuntz." Kujo held out his hand. "Call me Kujo."

Allie shook it, her brows raised. "Should I be afraid of your bite?"

Hank laughed. "Kuntz...Joe. Ku...Jo."

Allie nodded. "I get it. Nice to meet you. And this is?" She went down on her haunches to pet Six.

"Six," Kujo said.

She looked up. "That's his name?"

"It's the last number on his tattoo," Kujo explained and turned to Swede. "Need your help hacking into this." He held up the computer case.

"Let's do this inside." Hank held open the door.

Swede took the laptop case and followed Hank inside.

Molly gave him Daisy's birthdate. While Swede opened the computer and entered several combinations of Daisy's birthday numbers, Molly and Kujo filled

Hank in on the details of what had happened at Daisy's apartment.

"Apparently, someone is worried about the information on Tanner Birge's laptop," Kujo said.

"Daisy said Tanner's been working out at Pinion Ranch," Molly said. "Can you show me where that is on a map?"

Hank's brows furrowed. "Pinion Ranch butts up against the National Forest and the Crazy Mountains."

He led them into another part of the house and a large office with a huge mahogany desk in the middle. In the far corner of the office was a storage cabinet with wide, shallow drawers. Hank pulled one out, pushed it back in and slid out another. He lifted a huge square map from the drawer. "I got copies of all the survey maps available in the area around Oak Creek Ranch, my current home, and Bear Creek Ranch, my family's home. The Pinion Ranch borders Bear Creek on the southern border."

He pointed to the map. "On its eastern border is the highway, and the western edge backs up to the national forest." Hank hurried back to a drafting table and returned with a crumpled contour map.

"I recognize that map." Molly stepped forward and helped Hank flatten it. "This was the map I was using to search the surrounding areas."

"You were really close to the Pinion Ranch when you were flying your drone."

"Were you able to recover the footage on the drone's camera?" Kujo asked.

"Sadly, no," Hank shook his head. "The bullet hit the video storage device."

Molly sighed. "I still have to explain that one to my supervisor."

"Already have. He's more worried about having sent you here without a partner. I assured him we've got you covered."

Molly's cheeks bloomed with color. "I appreciate that."

Kujo's body warmed at the words. She was covered all right. He wondered what his new boss would think about just how well-covered Molly was. He changed the subject. "Did you get anything from the nomenclature on the board?"

"I hadn't before dinner. I sent it off to a friend of mine in procurement at the Pentagon earlier today." Hank turned to a computer monitor on a desk against the wall and wiggled the mouse. The black screen flooded with color. He clicked a few keys and brought up his email.

After scrolling through a couple screens, he stopped. "Wait. He responded." Hank leaned closer, his brows lowering. "Huh. Apparently, that box was a crate of M4A1 rifles that went missing from a warehouse near Ft. Drum, NY. They conducted an investigation of the warehouse employees. One went missing before they could interview him. He was found dead a couple days later."

"So, we might be dealing with some illegally acquired military weapons appropriated by people who aren't afraid to kill to keep anyone from spilling the beans," Kujo summarized.

Hank stood and faced Kujo and Molly. "Based on the sniper activity around Tanner Birge's arrest, I'd say the same type of people are at work here. Anxious to keep their secrets."

Molly nodded. "What can we do now?"

"Until Swede finds more information on that computer, not much."

"We need to look everywhere Tanner Birge has been. I want to get boots on the ground on Pinion Ranch," Molly said. "I'd say let's go tonight, but we wouldn't see much in the dark." Her gaze shot to Kujo. "Tomorrow? We can be there early in the morning."

He shook his head. "If it's truly a terrorist training camp, they will be on guard and watching for intruders. If they're planning anything soon, security will be even tighter. Especially if one of their trainees has gone rogue."

Hank nodded. "I can gather four or five members of the Brotherhood Protectors team, and we can stage a recon mission into the ranch."

"How soon?" Kujo asked.

Hank glanced at his watch. "Tomorrow." He held up his hand. "Depending on what we find on that computer, if anything."

Kujo nodded. "I like the plan."

Molly frowned. "You are including me on this mission onto the ranch, right?"

Hank glanced across Molly to Kujo.

Kujo tilted his head. "She's the reason we're even contemplating it. I say she's in."

"I'll gather the equipment we'll need," Hank said. "Be here at O-five-hundred in the morning. We'll need to brief the team regarding the communications devices and protocol for the mission."

Kujo's pulse hummed in anticipation. This was the kind of work he'd been trained for, the type of job he was good at. Though he'd included Molly, he wasn't sure she had as much cover and concealment training and tactical experience as the rest of Hank's team. Lack of training and experience got people killed. He'd talk to her on their way back to the B&B. Maybe he could talk her out of going.

Ha. Fat chance. The woman had a stubborn streak almost as long as his.

"In the meantime, you better get some rest." Hank glanced around at Molly. "You two are welcome to stay here for the night since you'll need to be here at the crack of dawn."

Molly shook her head. "No, thanks. We can be here that early." She didn't meet Kujo's gaze, and her face flushed pink.

Could it be she wanted to be alone with him through the night to pick up where they'd left off?

Kujo's groin tightened. "We'll be here at O-five-hundred. If you find anything tonight, call. We'll be available at a moment's notice."

Molly nodded.

They left Hank's office and passed Swede banging

away on the keyboard of the laptop. He didn't even glance up when Kujo and Molly walked by.

Allie lay on the couch nearby, her feet tucked beneath a blanket. "Hope to see you two soon," she said.

"Are you staying the night?" Molly asked.

"I haven't decided. I might leave him here. I have animals to take care of on Bear Creek Ranch in the morning. Dad can't do it all himself, anymore. We'd love it if you stopped by sometime. The gate's always open to friends of Hank's."

Hank held the door for Molly and Kujo. Six trotted out and went straight to Kujo's truck where he sat and waited for his master.

The trip back to the B&B passed in silence, Kujo thinking about what they'd learned, and the night ahead, potentially spent holding Molly in his arms. God, he hoped she was thinking along the same lines, or he'd spend a long time in a cold shower.

CHAPTER 15

MOLLY WAS first in the door at the B&B. Her heart raced, pounding an irregular beat against her ribs. She and Kujo had already had sex once. It wasn't as if it was an all-new experience for her.

Then why did she feel like a teen on her first date?

Kujo held the door for her but didn't follow her inside. "I'm going to exercise Six for a few minutes. I'll be in shortly."

Molly's excited heart slipped like a hunk of lead into her belly. She schooled her face to an indifferent mask in an attempt to hide her disappointment.

"Yeah. Sure." She nodded. "He's been patient with all of our running around all day. I'm sure he could use some exercise. I'll just go up." God, she sounded pathetic.

"We won't be long." Kujo caught her hand and tugged gently, pulling her up against him. "I promise." Then he pressed his lips to hers in a warm, hard kiss, before he let go.

Molly spun away, her cheeks flushed, her body on fire. All due to one single, tongue-less kiss. She might have burst into flames if he'd done more. She skipped up the stairs, a sense of joy in her heart and anticipation sending electrical impulses across her nerve endings.

She slipped into the shower for a quick rinse, rubbed soft-scented lotion on her body and scrounged through her suitcase for a pretty nightgown, remembering at the last minute she'd only brought T-shirts and shorts to sleep in. She'd planned a mission, not a seduction.

With a sigh, she pulled a soft gray T-shirt over her head. It hung down past her thighs, covering everything that needed covering, including the fact she hadn't put on any panties.

She creamed at her own naughtiness and couldn't wait for Kujo to discover her secret.

She glanced at the clock. Eight minutes had passed and still no Kujo. Molly bit her bottom lip. Should she go look for him? What if someone had come after him? What if he and Six were lying in the street bleeding out?

Molly jumped into a pair of jeans, tugged on her boots and ran for the door. As she reached for it, the handle twisted, and Kujo appeared with Six at his side, panting.

"Sorry, I didn't mean to keep you up. Six was more than happy for the exercise and didn't want to come back inside." Kujo stared down at her in her big T-shirt, jeans and boots. "Were you worried?"

"Of course, I was worried. After being shot at and having a cabin burn to the ground, I'm a little punchy. I thought maybe my bad luck had rubbed off on you and

Six." She let out a long breath and stepped aside, allowing them to enter the room.

Kujo's mere presence made the room seem smaller. His broad shoulders filled the space and stole the air. Suddenly, Molly couldn't breathe. Her body quickened at his nearness, and her sex grew damp in expectation of what could come.

Six weaved his way through their legs and flopped onto the wooden floor.

Kujo stepped across the threshold, closed the door behind him. He laid his weapon on the dresser.

Molly handed over her pistol.

Kujo laid it beside his. Then he took Molly into his arms and kissed her.

Molly melted into his embrace, her body pressing against his. She curled her hands around his neck and pulled him closer, opening her mouth to his insistent tongue. For a long moment, they stood frozen in that kiss, tongues caressing, hearts beating in sync.

When at last Kujo lifted his head, Molly remembered to breathe. But not for long.

Kujo scooped her up and strode for the bed.

"Don't trip on Six," Molly warned.

The dog saw them coming and moved out of the way.

Kujo set Molly on her feet, instead of the bed, ran his hands down her arms and grabbed the hem of her shirt, tugging it up her torso.

She raised her arms over her head and gazed into his eyes until he pulled the shirt over her head and tossed it onto a chair.

His lips curved into a smile when he saw she wasn't wearing a bra. He cupped her breasts in his palms. "Beautiful."

Molly laughed, her breath catching. "I'm up here," she joked.

Kujo raised his gaze to hers, and he gave her a slow, heart-stopping smile. "Yes, indeed, you are." He dragged her against him and kissed her, melding his mouth to hers. He gently ran his hands down her naked back, avoiding her injuries, and slipped his fingers beneath the waistband of her jeans.

The urgency of her need made her push him away.

He frowned down at her. "What's wrong?"

"You're wearing too many clothes. I'm wearing too many clothes, and we're wasting time." She pulled his shirt up over his body, admiring the defined muscles of his torso. Maybe she stared a little too long. He took over, ripping the garment over his head and dropping it to the floor.

"You're right. Too many clothes between us." His voice was a low, sexy growl. He stared up at her hungrily as he knelt to remove her boots and unbutton her jeans. Then he slid the denim over her hips and down her legs, taking his sweet time, as he touched her, brushing his knuckles across her skin, torturing as he descended to her ankles.

Once she was completely naked, he stood and Molly took control. She flicked the button loose on his jeans.

Kujo toed off his boots.

Hooking her thumbs into the waistband of his jeans, Molly dragged them down his thighs. She dropped to her knees to ease the fabric all the way down to his ankles.

Kujo stepped out of the jeans and kicked them to the side. He gripped her arms and attempted to pull her to her feet.

Molly shook her head, refusing to come up. Her eyes were on the prize.

She wrapped her hand around his engorged cock, amazed at how hard, long and thick he was. "Damn, Kujo, you're a freakin' stud."

He laughed out loud. "You do that to me."

Molly flicked her tongue across the velvety smooth head.

His shaft jerked in response and, a droplet of come emerged. "I'm not sure I have another condom," he said through tight lips. "But I'm clean of STDs."

"And I'm on the pill. So, what's the problem?" Molly took his dick in her mouth, clutched his tight ass in both hands, and sucked him in until he hit the back of her throat.

Kujo caressed the top of her head, weaving his fingers into her hair. "Keep that up and I won't last long."

Molly leaned back, letting his shaft slide all the way out of her, her hand replacing her mouth around him. "I take it you like that."

"You have no idea."

She squeezed him gently. "I think I have an idea." Then she took him into her mouth again, flicking the tip and gliding her tongue around the ridge.

Kujo fisted his hand in her hair and held her head as he thrust into her mouth.

Molly dug her fingernails into his buttocks and forced him deeper. His firm, velvety thickness in her mouth made her want him inside her, or at least touching her aching entrance.

"Much as I love what you're doing, I want to touch you, too." Kujo pulled out of her mouth, scooped her off the floor and laid her on the bed.

When he climbed onto the bed, she moved toward the center

"I wasn't finished," she complained.

"And I haven't started." He straddled her head with his knees and bent over her body to part her folds with his thumbs. "Now, we're on equal footing."

"Mmm." She sucked his cock into her mouth as he came down on her and licked her clitoris, sending her into waves of ecstasy. She raised her knees, planted her heels in the mattress and rose to meet his glorious tongue.

While she sucked him, he flicked her nubbin until she was squirming beneath him, her body stiffening until that excruciatingly moment when she exploded into an orgasm that rocked her world.

Kujo continued the attack until Molly had wrung every last little bit of sensation out of her release. But it wasn't enough. She had to have him inside her, down there, filling that empty space so exquisitely sensitive after he'd brought her to the brink of sanity and back.

Molly pushed him away, forcing him to lie on his back. "My turn to do the work."

"I thought you were."

"Baby, I've only just begun." She climbed on top of him, straddled his hips and positioned her entrance over the tip of his cock. "Are you ready?" She lowered herself just enough to wet the tip of his shaft.

"Yes!" He raised his hips, dipping in.

Molly came down on him and rose back up. She repeated the motion, moving faster and faster.

Kujo gripped her hips and brought her down harder as he thrust upward. Then he lifted her off him and set her on the bed beside him.

She frowned. "But you weren't there, yet."

"I want to go deeper, harder and faster."

Her pussy creamed, and she smiled. "I'm all for it."

"Good." He rose on his knees and flipped her onto her stomach.

Molly hadn't expected the movement, but understood when he gripped her hips and raised her bottom into the air.

Then he kneed her legs apart and settled on his behind her. He leaned over her back and cupped her breasts, squeezing gently. "I want to fuck you hard and fast. Any objections, tell me now."

His rich, rough tones slid over her like melted butter, sliding into every part of her being. "Please," she said and rose on her hands.

Kujo thrust into her. As good as his word, he fucked her hard and fast, again and again.

The friction and pounding sent Molly back up that peak, until she was teetering on the edge.

She dropped her chest to the mattress, freeing one of

her hands to touch herself. She flicked her own clit as Kujo filled her inside. The combination shot her over the top, and she climaxed, her body shaking with the intensity.

Kujo slammed into her once more and held her hips tight, his cock buried deeply inside her, throbbing with his release.

After many long moments, Kujo eased Molly onto her belly and rolled with her to his side, spooning her body, his cock still rock-hard within her. One of his hands circled around her, toying with her breast.

Molly lay nestled against him, her backside warmed by his front, their intimate connection incredibly reassuring. "Joe?" she whispered.

"Yeah, babe."

"Are you thinking about tomorrow?"

"I'm thinking about how beautiful you are, and how good you feel." He squeezed her breast and pinched the nipple between his thumb and fingers.

"Mmm," she murmured. She let her thoughts leave her for a moment, but they came back to haunt. "When we find the ISIS training camp, then what?"

"We bring in the big guns to close them down." Kujo leaned close and nibbled her ear. "Then we celebrate by doing this." He pumped into her with his still-hard cock.

She covered his hand with hers and pressed her bottom backward, taking more of his length. God, he felt good inside her. But she couldn't shake her dread of the future. "What about after we close them down? What then?" She hadn't asked him for commitment when they'd first made love. And she wouldn't ask him now.

"I'm sure Hank will assign me to another client."

"And I'll be on my way back to DC," she murmured.

His hand on her breast stilled for a long moment. Then he palmed her breast. "I hadn't thought that far ahead."

"I hadn't either, until now." What did she expect him to say? Did she want him to declare his undying love for her, after knowing her for so short a time? A dull ache grew in the pit of her belly. No. Love was too soon. And they wouldn't get the opportunity to find out.

Her throat thickened, and she swallowed hard before saying, "I need a glass of water. Can I get you anything while I'm downstairs?"

"I'll go," he said.

"No, please. I need to stretch my legs." She slipped from his arms, his cock sliding from her body. When she stood, she grabbed for her T-shirt, pulled it over her head, and jammed her legs into her jeans.

Kujo swung his legs over the side of the bed. "I'll come with you."

"No, please. I need some...space," she said.

He frowned. "Is it something I said? Because, if it was, I don't know what it could be. Please. Come back to bed, and I'll make it up to you, whatever it was that's made you unhappy."

She smiled at him, her eyes burning with tears she wouldn't let fall. To hide them from him, she turned away, pretending to search for her shoes. "No, no. I'm not mad, or anything. It's just that everything is moving so fast, and I just don't want to do anything I'll regret." She gave him a sideways smile. "I'll be right back."

She gave up on the shoes and headed for the door. As she passed Six, the dog rose from the floor to follow her.

"Six, stay," Kujo commanded.

The dog immediately lay on the floor between Kujo and Molly and rested his chin on his front paws, staring at Molly as she neared the door. Six rolled his eyes toward Kujo, his face seeming to plead with his master.

Molly would have laughed if she weren't already struggling to breathe past the tightness in her throat. "Oh, please, if he wants, I can take him out for one last time before we call it a night."

Kujo shrugged. "If you're sure he won't bother you."

"Not at all." Molly held the door open for the dog. "Six, come," she said with the same amount of force she'd heard from Kujo.

The dog remained where he was, his gaze darting from Molly back to Kujo.

Kujo nodded. "Six, go."

Six leaped to his feet and ran for the door, his butt and tail wiggling so fast he could barely stand still.

No matter how sad Molly felt, Six's happiness wouldn't let her be down for long. "You're a good boy, Six." She scratched behind his ears, cast a glance at his owner and sucked in a deep breath.

The man rose from the bed, naked, and so damned gorgeous, he brought more tears to Molly's eyes and heat throughout her body.

"I'll be back," she choked out, turned and ran down

the stairs barefooted, Six right behind her. She hurried out of the B&B into the chilly, night air, the concrete sidewalk cool against her toes.

Six bounded outside, ran for the nearest post and relieved himself.

Molly sucked in deep breaths, willing her pulse and her core temperature to calm. She stood for a long time until she shivered, her bare arms and feet reminding her of how cold the nights could be in the Crazy Mountains.

"Six, come," she called out.

Six immediately returned to her side, sat and stared up at her, his tongue lolling to one side, his eager gaze fixed on hers.

Molly opened the front door to the B&B and held it for Six to enter.

The dog leaped inside and turned looking at her for a moment.

Molly hesitated, suddenly nervous and shy about returning to the bedroom she'd share with the man who'd wrung the most intense orgasm out of her body ever.

She'd told him she needed space. Hell, what if he thought she wanted him to get lost? That was the last thing she wanted. If anything, she wanted to tell him she would give up everything to be with him. Even her job with the FBI, if only he wanted her as much as she wanted him.

Molly also knew that if she said anything like that, he'd run in the opposite direction as fast as his sexy legs would carry him. Nothing sent a man running faster than a declaration of love so soon after a woman met him.

Six stared at her, standing in the doorway.

"Yeah, I know. I'm completely irrational," she said aloud to the dog.

In response, Six emitted a low, threatening growl.

"What's wrong, Six?" Molly asked. A shiver trickled down her spine. She leaned toward the doorway when an arm snaked out and wrapped around her trunk, trapping her arms against her sides. A meaty hand clamped tightly over her mouth. She was yanked backward. The B&B door hinge, which hung on a spring, retracted, slamming the door shut, Six trapped inside, with a finality that made Molly's heart slip into her belly.

She tried to scream, but nothing more than a desperate murmur made it past the thick hand covering her mouth.

On the other side of the door, Six barked and scratched in an attempt to get to her.

Molly fought, kicked and wiggled, but the arm around her was strong. She stomped on the man's instep. He grunted and slammed an open palm against her temple, knocking the sense out of her head and sending her into a gray and black spinning vortex that sucked her into an ever-darkening hell.

CHAPTER 16

Kujo dressed in jeans and a T-shirt and pulled on his boots. He clipped the satellite phone onto his belt. If Molly wanted space, he could go for a walk with Six.

He paced the room several times, counting the minutes until Molly's return. How much space was enough? And how did that translate into time? Was she rethinking their microburst of a relationship? Did she regret making love with him? Shit, had she faked her orgasm just to get it over with?

He shook his head. *No way.* Her body had been as tense as his, and her tremors had appeared uncontrolled.

With a glance at his watch, he tucked his pistol into the waistband of his jeans and stared at the door, willing Molly to enter. Five minutes had passed since she'd left the room. As far as he was concerned, that was long enough. Kujo's hand was on the doorknob when Six started barking.

Kujo's heart thudded against his ribs. He yanked open the door and ran to the head of the stairs.

Six was at the screen door, tearing at the mesh with his paws, frantically trying to break through to get outside.

By the time Kujo made it to the bottom of the staircase, Mrs. K had emerged in her bathrobe with her hair up in sponge curlers, blinking the sleep from her eyes. "What's going on? My Lord, why is Six destroying my door?"

He didn't respond, just powered past her, opened the door and ran outside.

Six shot ahead of him, racing down the street after the disappearing taillights of what appeared to be a truck turning onto Main Street.

Kujo could think of only one reason Six would be chasing the truck.

Molly.

Mrs. K came out of the B&B behind him.

As he ran to his truck, Kujo yelled, "Call 911. Molly's been abducted. She might be in a pickup. I'm going after her." He jumped into the driver's seat and cranked the engine. He was halfway down the street in seconds.

Six cut through a yard, leaped over a low bush and ran like the wind.

By the time Kujo reached the corner, the taillights were near the edge of town. Six ran down the middle of the street, losing ground on the disappearing truck.

Kujo raced after them. When he came alongside the slowing dog, he flung open his door and yelled. "Six, come!" The dog shot a glance toward him and then back at the truck, so far ahead. As if making up his mind, he slowed long enough to jump up into the truck, clambering over Kujo to the passenger seat. Once there, he sat forward, his gaze on the road in front of them, his tongue lolling from his mouth as he gasped for air.

Kujo closed his door and slammed his foot to the accelerator. He'd have to push it to catch the other vehicle. And he didn't know for certain Molly was in it. What he did know was Molly had been taken. He knew in his gut she wouldn't have gone walking alone, leaving Six in the house.

He switched off his headlights and focused on the taillights in front of him, doing his best to catch up to the truck and yet, not be seen. He pulled the satellite phone off his belt and hit the numbers for Hank.

Hank answered after the second ring. "Kujo, what's wrong?"

"Molly's been taken. I'm following a pickup I think she might be in. The B&B owner is putting a call through to 911. I might need help."

"I'm in the process of gathering the team. Which way are you headed?"

"East, into the Crazy Mountains." He told him the highway number and the direction. "I'm flying in stealth-mode with my lights out. I don't think he knows he's being followed.

"As I said, I was in the process of gathering the team, anyway, and I was about to call you," Hank said.

"Why?"

"Swede found a social media group Tanner Birge belonged to called TA for Take America. On the page, we found images of weapons, political statements against the current administration and more."

"That doesn't mean they're plotting a coup."

"No, but there were several passages that seemed to be encoded messages. I had Swede and Molly's boss, Pete, work on decoding. It didn't take long. Apparently, they're planning something big in the next couple of days. They put out a call to all their disciples, as they call themselves. And they end the messages in AA."

Kujo's blood ran cold. "Allah Akbar." The cry most jihadists called out as they killed non-believers of Islam. *God is greatest.*

"That's not all. The owner of the ranch has been missing for several months. Supposedly, he left on a vacation to Mexico. He hasn't been heard from since."

"Great. A missing woman, a missing ranch owner and ISIS training leaders calling their forces together for a big operation." Kujo laughed, humor absent from the sound. "Any more good news for me?"

"Four of the team members are on their way out to the ranch now. We can be at your location within fifteen minutes."

"I'm not waiting. If they're planning something big, they might not let Molly live long enough for the team to get in there and free her."

"Do what you have to, but don't get yourself killed. We'll be there as soon as we can. I'm mobilizing now. I'll meet the team on the road. Do you still have your GPS tracker on you?"

"I do," Kujo said.

"Good. If you get to a point you can't communicate,

we'll follow your blip on the screen. Kujo, we've got your back."

Kujo felt the sense of belonging he'd missed since he'd been cashiered out of the military. That feeling of family, a community of people who understood him and his way of thinking. "Thanks."

The brake lights on the truck ahead of him blinked red as the vehicle slowed and turned off the highway onto a side road.

Though the darkness changed his perspective, Kujo could tell this road was the one leading onto Pinion Ranch.

They should have gotten out there sooner, uncovered the ISIS training activities and shut them down before Molly was taken.

Now, he had nothing but his wits to guide him through what might happen. The team wouldn't be there before he had to ditch his own truck and follow on foot.

He prayed Molly was all right. If they hurt her, he'd make them pay with their lives.

His fists clenched around the steering wheel as he neared the turnoff onto the dirt road leading across a cattle guard onto the ranch with the missing owner.

Kujo couldn't be sure the entrance wasn't being monitored. He pulled past the turnoff. When he reached a bend in the road, he waited until he was past it to apply his brakes to keep anyone watching from the Pinion Ranch entrance from seeing his brake lights flare.

He pulled the truck off the road, hiding it behind

bushes and trees. Then he snapped a lead on Six and got out. Kujo reached into the back of the cab for the rifle he kept in a case behind the back seat. Shoving boxes of bullets into his pockets, he straightened and closed the door. From this point, he'd be on foot.

He just hoped he could cover enough ground fast enough to be there in time to help Molly.

Kujo took off at a jog, carrying his rifle and encouraging Six to find the truck he'd been chasing.

MOLLY CAME to when her head bounced against what felt like a rubber mat. She opened her eyes and stared around at what appeared to be the cab of a pickup truck. She lay jammed between the front and back seats on the floorboard. The scent of dust and diesel fuel filled her nostrils, making her want to sneeze. She wiggled her nose, willing herself to hold off long enough to figure out an escape plan. If her captor knew she was awake, he might hit her again.

She lowered her eyelids and, peering through her lashes, looked around the interior, searching for a quick exit. If she could reach the door handle above her, she could open it, do a flip and roll out the side.

The likelihood of success was minimal. She'd have to be a contortionist to flip over backward while jammed between the front and the back seat on the floorboard.

Her head pounded, her left temple aching from where the man had hit her, but she couldn't give up, nor could she let him win. When she got the chance, she'd give the bastard what he deserved and more.

Molly used every time the vehicle bumped over a big rut to shift her body until she lay on her belly. If she played her cards right, she could use the next bump to shift her knees beneath her. The driver might see her bottom rise from the floorboard, but by then she might be able to get her hands on the door handle, shove it open and propel herself out of the truck. Then all she had to do was to survive the landing, pick herself up and run into the woods. Being lost in the woods wasn't nearly as concerning as being in the clutches of someone who'd knocked her unconscious and carried her away from the B&B and Kujo.

Another bump gave her enough momentum to lunge for the handle. She grabbed it and shoved the door open, pushed hard and flung herself out onto the ground.

She fell hard, landing on her shoulder. Pain shot through her arm. Molly couldn't worry about it, she had to keep going. Rolling away from the truck and the tires, she pushed to her feet.

The truck ground to a halt behind her. A door opened and a man jumped down. "Goddamn, bitch. You'll be sorry."

He caught her before her vision cleared, and she could take ten steps. Grabbing her by her hair, he dragged her backward.

Instead of trying to run and risk losing a hank of hair, she backed into him, fast and hard, knocking him off balance. He let go of her hair and fell on his ass.

Unfortunately, so did Molly, landing in the middle of the man's belly.

Air blasted from his lungs.

For the moment, he lay there. Molly struggled to get her feet beneath her and shot to a standing position.

A hand clamped on her ankle.

She tried to raise her foot, but the hand around her ankle kept her from going far.

Molly turned and slammed her heel into the man's face. "Take that, you son of a bitch." She heard the satisfying crunch of cartilage breaking in his nose.

The man jerked his hands back to cover his face, spewing curse words muffled by his hand.

Once again, Molly turned to run but hit the brick wall of someone's chest, bringing her up short. Hands gripped her arms and a familiar face stared down into hers. "Why the hell did you bring her?"

Molly gazed into the face of David Perez, the real estate agent who'd shown her and Kujo around the county, searching for properties for sale.

"I don't understand," she whispered. "What are you doing here?

"That's not as important as your reason for being here," He grabbed the front of her shirt and pulled her up against him.

"Trust me, I don't want to be here. That man hit me and shoved me into his truck. Ask him why." She glanced around at the view in the darkness. Several electric lanterns had been lit, but it was the tents beneath the camouflage netting that made her pulse quicken.

Men stood beside trucks loaded with wooden crates. One by one, they handed out weapons, in many sizes and shapes. Most appeared to be military-grade rifles and machine guns. Another man passed around vests, and yet another distributed hand grenades.

From what Molly could tell, they were gearing up for war. Only they weren't US military forces. They appeared to be a bunch of bearded bubbas, some younger, angry looking men of a variety of ethnic backgrounds and a few men Molly had seen in Eagle Rock recently.

Perez nodded to the bearded man who'd gotten out of the truck. "Diener, why is she here?"

"I owed her boyfriend for making my wife leave me."

Perez's mouth twisted into a snarl. "You realize what bringing her here means?"

Diener smirked. "It means she can't leave. She'll have to die. Serves that Kuntz fellow right."

"It also means her fiancé will be searching for her. You've raised the chances of being discovered before we've completed our mission." Perez nodded to one of the men standing nearby. "The penalty for revealing our location to outsiders is clearly outlined in the training."

"Hey." Diener raised his hands and backed away, his eyes widening. "I did you a favor by bringing her here. She's the one who was snooping in the valley the other day." He shouted to another man. "Birge, tell 'em."

A clean-shaven younger man stepped away from his position handing out grenades to others. He carried one of the grenades in his palm as he approached Perez and Diener. "What are you talking about?"

Diener glared at Birge. "Tell Mohammed about the

person you thought you shot in the valley. The one who was flying the drone."

Birge shrugged. "I shot down a drone in the valley and chased someone on a four-wheeler. So?"

"So? You thought it might be her, the woman who was shackin' up with the stranger in the old DeLong hunting cabin in the woods."

"Again." The younger man stared at Diener with a deadpan face, no emotion nor expression in his eyes or anywhere else. "I don't know what you're talking about. I figured whoever was flying that drone shouldn't be snooping in the valley when we were still moving supplies. So, I took care of it."

Molly stared into the eyes of Daisy's ex-boyfriend and struggled not to let a shiver shake her entire body. The man appeared to have no soul whatsoever.

Diener's eyes narrowed. "That's not what you told me. And I suppose you didn't bother to tell Mohammed it was you who set that explosive at Al's Diner."

Molly couldn't see Perez's expression, but she felt him stiffen behind her.

"Birge, were you the one behind the explosion in town earlier today?" Perez demanded.

Birge shook his head. "Why would I start something that could bring in the ATF, the FBI and the National Guard? That would undermine our mission. I'm not that stupid."

"You lying bastard." Diener lunged for Birge and slugged him in the face.

Molly clenched her fists. Birge was lying and deserved to be slugged. He'd almost killed Al and his ex-girlfriend was in the hospital. If she could Molly would have put a bullet between the jerk's eyes.

Birge staggered backward, clutching at his jaw. "I'm not the one interested in revenge. I didn't burn down a hunting cabin to kill the man who broke up a fight between my old lady and me."

Diener pointed at Birge. "No, but you planted the explosives to take out your girlfriend who worked at the diner."

"From what I heard, the man who broke up the fight between you and your wife was inside that diner when the explosives went off. I have no interest in hurting Daisy. We've been done for a long time. She just did me a favor by moving all of my stuff out of her apartment."

Perez's grip tightened on Molly's arm. "And by all your stuff, are you referring to furniture and clothing? What about your computer? Can you tell me where your laptop is at this very moment?"

In the light from the open door of the truck, Molly could see Birge's face pale. But he raised his chin. "It's in my vehicle."

"Liar!" Diener shouted. "Daisy had it. When you went to get it, someone got there before you."

Birge's lip curled back in a snarl. "You don't know that."

"I was there. I saw you go into her apartment. I also saw someone sneak into her car and take the computer bag."

"Since your vehicle is here, Birge," Perez said, his tone low and threatening, "be so good as to show me your laptop."

Birge turned and started to walk away. He took only five steps and then broke into a run, veering toward the woods.

Diener raised the pistol in his hand and shot Birge in the back.

Birge staggered and fell, face first, to the ground, where he lay still.

"I told you he was lying."

Molly's heart thundered, but she had to play it cool. She was in enemy territory and the man holding her wasn't the friendly real estate agent she'd thought he was. Apparently, she'd found an ISIS training camp, and he was their leader, a man they called Mohammed.

So much for not engaging the enemy. *Now, would be a good time to come up with a backup plan.* She had to get out of the camp, back to town, and call for reinforcements.

The arm around her tightened. "Bind her," Mohammed commanded.

Diener smirked. "I told you she was worth capturing."

"You've caused enough trouble with your petty desire for revenge. Don't give me a reason to do to you what you did to Birge." He shoved Molly toward Diener, who caught her in one of his thick arms, crushing her against his side.

Molly cocked her elbow, ready to plant it in Diener's gut, but stopped when she stared down the barrel of a nine-millimeter Glock.

"All I have to do is pull the trigger and take care of

two thorns in my side." Mohammed's eyes narrowed into slits. "Go ahead. Tempt me."

Molly lowered her arm. She could fight people, but a bullet wasn't as easily overcome.

Perez's hand never wavered, but he raised his gaze to the man behind Molly. "We're moving our mission in Bozeman and Helena up a day."

Diener shifted his weight. "But we can't move all the supplies by morning."

"Then we'll take what we can and destroy the rest." Mohammed stared at Molly. "And by the rest, that includes you."

CHAPTER 17

KUJO RAN THROUGH THE WOODS, paralleling the road the truck had taken into Pinion Ranch, all the while ignoring the pain in his bum leg. The physical ache would eventually go away. The emotional anguish of Molly's death wouldn't be eased by putting his feet up. He had to reach her before her captor did anything to harm her.

Six ran alongside him, his unsteady gait not slowing him one bit. The dog had found a friend in Molly and seemed as concerned about her wellbeing as Kujo.

After what felt like miles, Kujo glimpsed a flicker of a light ahead, between the trees and brush.

He slowed, pulling Six to a stop. If what he was nearing was the ISIS training camp, there could be sentries guarding the perimeter.

Kujo knelt on the ground beside Six, unhooked the lead from the animal's collar and spoke quietly, but firmly near the dog's ear. "Heel."

Six sat on his haunches and waited for Kujo's next

command, his attention completely focused on his master. At that moment, he appeared to be the dog Kujo had partnered with in battle all those years ago.

He tested the theory by taking several steps through the woods.

Six trotted beside him, matching his pace.

With no time to waste, Kujo ducked low and worked his way toward the encampment then circled the area. The only guards he spotted were at the entrance, on either side of the road.

The site was nestled into the trees. Tents had been erected and covered with camouflage netting to blend into the foliage, making it difficult to spot from above. He counted twenty-eight men moving about, loading items into the backs of pickup trucks with short camper shells on the back. What didn't fit, they stacked in a pile at the center of the area between the tents.

Kujo wished he had his satellite phone to call Hank and warn him about the number of men in the camp. The four or five men his boss could round up from the Brotherhood Protectors would be no match against the number of men he was counting. And all Kujo had was his rifle and Six.

A man shouted, drawing Kujo's attention. Three men stood near the open door of a pickup. The interior light shining behind them made silhouettes out of their bodies. One of the men seemed thicker than the others until Kujo realized he was holding a body against him.

More shouting made Kujo strain to make out the words. But he was too far away. Then one of the men started to walk away. He didn't go far before he broke into a run.

The sharp report of gunfire sounded, and the running man dropped to the ground.

The man holding the body shoved it toward the one who'd fired the shot and walked away.

The shooter spun the person around and appeared to bind the figure to the pile of boxes and debris growing in the middle of the camp. With the headlights of a vehicle backlighting the figure, Kujo couldn't see a face, but he knew by the feminine shape, that person was Molly.

A twig snapped nearby.

Six growled low in his chest and hunkered down, ready to spring.

Kujo spun and dropped to a prone position, his arms out in front of him, his weapon pointed in the direction of the noise.

"Kujo," a voice whispered in the darkness. "Don't shoot me." Bear low-crawled to Kujo's position.

"Are you trying to get yourself killed?" Kujo gritted out.

"I was more worried about Six ripping off my face." Bear handed him a headset. "The gang's all here. Seven, counting you."

He didn't know how the hell they'd arrived so quickly, but he was glad they had his back.

"Hank checked with the sheriff. They're mobilizing and on their way here."

Kujo shook his head. "Can't wait for them. See the pile of boxes in the middle?"

"Yeah," Bear acknowledged.

"Molly's somewhere near that pile. They're loading the trucks. It looks like the pile is what they're leaving behind."

Bear stared at the center of the camp. "And they won't leave that much evidence intact."

Kujo's gut knotted. Bear's conclusion was what Kujo had come up with. Which meant when the trucks moved out, they'd set fire to, or detonate, what was left. "We have to get her out of there before that happens."

"Enemy head count?" Bear queried.

Kujo settled the headset over his head and pressed it into his ear. "Twenty-eight tangos."

"Four to one," Hank's voice came over the radio. "The odds are in our favor."

Kujo had been in operations where they'd had ten-to-one odds. Hope flared. "If you all could take the rest, I'll get Molly."

"Yeah, take the sweet job," Bear said. "Leave us with the bubbas."

"Let's do it," Hank said. "Keep it quiet, and only use necessary force. We're not in Afghanistan or Iraq."

"Your definition of necessary?" Duke said.

Hank didn't answer. The team moved forward, slipping into the camp on silent feet.

His concentration on Molly, Kujo nearly missed a man lounging in the shadows, his back to the wheel of a truck, sound asleep.

Six alerted Kujo with a low growl.

Kujo hit the guy in the temple with the grip of his pistol. The man went down without a fight, never waking up. He'd likely rouse to a sheriff's deputy reading his Miranda rights as he dragged the traitor's ass into the back of his service vehicle. Just to make sure, Kujo pulled the man's shirt over his head and tied his arms together behind his back. He didn't like taking the time to do it, but he couldn't risk the man sneaking up behind him when he was getting Molly out of trouble.

Kujo couldn't hear the team as they dealt with the men in the camp, but he trusted they'd be there if he needed assistance. He prayed he wasn't too late.

MOLLY STRUGGLED to loosen the zip-tie Diener had used to bind her ankles and to secure her wrists behind her back. Then he'd dragged her across camp and shoved her toward the growing stack of empty crates and boxes. Unable to catch herself, she fell against a wooden crate, hitting it with her hip.

That's going to leave a bruise, she thought as she glanced off the crate and did a face-plant in the dirt. She rolled to her side and used her elbow to leverage herself high enough she finally managed to sit up.

"Hurry it up! If it won't fit, we'll destroy it," Mohammed called out. "Five minutes, and we bug out."

The sense of urgency grew more frenetic until the men were throwing what they could into the truck beds, running from tents to trucks.

Molly scooted back against one of the crates and rubbed the zip-tie against an edge of rough wood.

"Come on," she muttered, rubbing harder, taking

layers of skin off her arms and wrists with each pass. Skin would grow back. But if she didn't get out of there soon, they'd light her up with the debris they left behind. And she needed to get back to civilization to warn law enforcement that these men were planning assaults in Bozeman and Helena the following morning. If she didn't get away and warn someone, innocent people would die.

With lives hanging in the balance, Molly rubbed harder, and, finally, the zip-tie snapped and her wrists were free. When none of the frantic men were looking, she broke a board off a crate, and twisted it into the zip-tie binding her ankles until it broke. She sprang to her feet and started for the safety of the woods.

"Oh, no you don't." Someone grabbed her hair and yanked backward, nearly pulling her off her feet. The barrel of a pistol pressed against her temple.

Instinct kicked in. Molly pushed her hand up between them, knocking his pistol upward.

He fired, the shot going into the air.

The sound of the gunshot threw the rest of the men into a panic. Suddenly there were more people than before, some of them fighting. More shots were fired, and men yelled.

Molly didn't have time to wonder what the heck was happening around her. She wrapped her arm around her attackers and twisted his behind his back, forcing him to drop the pistol. He lurched forward, taking her with him and falling to the ground.

Molly fell on top of him, refusing to release her hold

on the arm she'd shoved up between his shoulder blades.

Perez, or Mohammed, as Tanner and Diener had called him, rolled over, crushing her beneath him, his weight pushing the air from her lungs.

A flash of fur streaked from the right and leaped onto Mohammed. Six's deep, vicious growl might have frightened some, but to Molly, it was the sound of heaven.

Six ripped into Mohammed's arm, tearing into the flesh.

Mohammed cried out then rolled, kicked and flailed, but Six wouldn't let go.

When Mohammed's body slipped off Molly's, she rolled away and pushed to her feet.

"I should have killed you in town." Ray Diener stood in front of her, his pistol pointed at Molly's head.

Half crouching, Molly shivered with rage. She'd been so damn close. "Go ahead, shoot me. But you won't get away with this. The sheriff is on his way. You won't get to the highway before they catch you. You might as well give up."

"Shut up, bitch!" He lowered his weapon and pointed at her chest, but before he could pull the trigger, a shot rang out.

Diener dropped where he was, the gun falling from his hand onto the dirt.

Molly looked in the direction from where the shot had been fired.

Kujo stood with his pistol held out, his hand shaking. "Holy shit, Molly. I thought you were dead."

Molly straightened and glanced to the side. Six held Mohammed pinned to the ground.

With his free hand, Mohammed reached for the weapon Diener had dropped. When his fingers closed around it, he raised it, aiming toward Six.

"No fucking way." Molly kicked his hand so hard, the bone snapped and the gun flew into the pile of boxes. Mohammed screamed in pain.

Kujo raced to her side and pulled her into his arms.

Sirens wailed as the fighting came to an end.

The Brotherhood Protectors emerged victorious, the ISIS-trained men lying at their feet, holding broken limbs or hands to the gunshot wounds that had maimed but wouldn't kill.

"How did you find me?" Molly asked, leaning hard against his chest.

"I was right behind the truck he took you in, up until he turned down the road to the ranch." He pulled her closer and pressed his cheek to her hair. "I couldn't let them hurt you. You're the best thing to happen to me since I got Six back."

She laughed. "I see where I rank. First Six, and then me."

"How about equal?" He tilted her chin up and pressed his lips to hers for a quick, hard kiss.

"I can live with that," she whispered into his mouth. "You both saved my life. My heroes."

"You're a brave, woman, Molly Greenbriar." He kissed her again while Six growled and shook Mohammed's arm.

The sheriff, and every deputy in the county arrived,

along with the fire department and emergency medical technicians.

While the sheriff's deputies cuffed and read the ISIS trainees their rights, Molly gave the sheriff the rundown on Mohammed's plans to wreak havoc on Bozeman and Helena. Hank told him about the information they'd hacked from Birge's laptop and promised to hand it over as evidence.

Hank gathered the Brotherhood Protectors and Molly in a half-circle away from the melee.

"You all did well tonight. I've cleared it with the sheriff to cut loose. He'll want to get statements from you, but we need to get out of here before the media descends on us."

"But that would be good advertisement for the team," Duke said.

"Yeah," Bear agreed. "You'd get more business."

Hank grinned. "I've got more business than I have men to work. Looks like we'll be hiring more people." He pounded Kujo on the back. "And you've more than proven yourself as part of this team." He held out his hand to Kujo. "Welcome aboard, Kujo. Glad you're part of Brotherhood Protectors."

Kujo shook his boss's hand. "Thanks, but Six gets the credit for saving Molly. He and I are a team."

"Absolutely." Hank dropped to one knee and held out his hand to Six, now that the dog had been relieved of his prey. "Welcome to the team, Six."

Six put his paw in Hank's hand and barked.

The team laughed and congratulated each other on a

job well done. Then they headed back to the highway where they'd left their vehicles.

Kujo insisted Molly get the EMTs to treat the wounds on her wrists and hip and check her for concussion. When they cleared her, he lifted her into his arms and carried her back down the road to where he'd left his truck.

"You know I can walk, right?"

He nodded. "I know." But he carried her all the way to the truck and settled her in the passenger seat.

They were back at the B&B twenty minutes later. Molly made the trip in silence, wondering what was next between her and Kujo. Before she was abducted, she'd wanted space to think, to get her mind around her growing attraction to the man.

After all that had happened, all she wanted now was to be in his arms.

Mrs. K met them at the door. "I've been listening to the scanner. I'm so glad you're all right."

"I'm sorry about the door, Mrs. K," Kujo said.

The older woman waved her hand. "Now, don't you worry about that. I'm just glad Miss Molly is okay." She hugged them both and promised a big breakfast in the morning to celebrate their return.

Molly climbed the stairs and entered their room. She waited for Kujo to close the door, and then she threw herself into his arms.

"Hey," he said, brushing the hair back from her face. "What's this? I thought you wanted space." He chuckled. "How's that going for you?"

"I'm done with space. I want you," she said. "I don't

know if you feel the same, but I'll take any scrap of attention you want to throw my way. If you feel the same, I'll make it work somehow. We can make a long-distance relationship work, can't we? I can fly out whenever I have time off. Better yet, I can transfer to the Montana office of the FBI. We can do this." She looked up at him, her eyes filling with tears. "Please say something. I know I'm making a complete fool of myself."

He cupped her cheeks in his hands and bent to kiss her forehead.

Molly's heart sank to her knees. A man didn't kiss a woman's forehead unless he was about to break up with her.

She braced herself for the pain, knowing it would be worse than any wound she'd ever received.

Kujo arched an eyebrow. "Now that I can get a word in edgewise, I want to say, I'll give you the space you need as long as it never exceeds five minutes again. I almost lost my mind waiting for you to come back to the room. I'd given up on waiting, and was about to beg you to come back, when Six started barking."

She stared up into his eyes, her heart swelling, tears tipping over the edges of her eyes and trailing down her cheeks.

He nodded. "I don't know how I went from a mountain hermit to falling in love with a woman in less than a week, but here I am, my heart in your hands. Give me a chance to show you how much you mean to me. Go on a date with me. Let me woo you the way you deserve. Will you let me love you?"

"Yes!" Molly stood on her toes and kissed him like there might be no tomorrow. And that had almost been the case.

Kujo held her close, loving her back as hard as she was loving him.

Six pressed his warm, furry body against them, making their joy complete.

EPILOGUE

KUJO STOOD on the porch looking out over his valley. The Crazy Mountains rose behind him, and the blue Montana sky was bright and clear above. Molly was in the yard, throwing a ball for Six to keep the dog's injured leg from getting stiff.

They'd found the cabin in the mountains a few weeks ago and made an offer. The owner, who'd moved to Florida, accepted. The timing couldn't have been better.

Molly's transfer to the FBI's regional office had been denied. Her boss, Pete, wanted to keep her and arranged for her to take field assignments from her new home in Montana.

Molly tossed the ball one last time for Six and climbed up to stand beside Kujo on the deck.

He slipped his arm around her waist and pulled her against his body. "The team will be here in a few minutes. Are you ready to host our first barbeque at our new place?"

She nodded. "I can't believe this is ours." She grinned up at him. "I keep thinking life can't get any better just being with you, but then it does."

"I know what you mean. But I can think of one more thing to make it better."

"Yeah?" She leaned up on her toes. "Like maybe a kiss?" She pressed her lips to his, but he only gave her a brief peck then set her back on her heels.

"Yes, to the kiss, but that wasn't quite what I had in mind." He dug in his pocket for what he'd gone all the way to Helena to find. When his fingers wrapped around the object, he took her hand and dropped down to one knee.

Molly frowned. "What are you doing?"

"Molly Greenbriar, we've known each other now for three months, four days, ten hours and thirty-seven minutes."

Her eyes rounded and filled with tears. "You're not—oh, hell—is this...?"

"Shut up and listen," he said. "I don't want another minute to go by that you aren't mine. Will you marry me?"

"Yes! Oh, yes. Please." Molly dropped down on her knees and curled her fingers around his.

He pried his hand loose and slipped the ring onto her finger. "The sooner we start the rest of our lives, the better."

IF YOU ENJOYED THIS STORY, you might enjoy others in the:

Brotherhood Protectors Series
Montana SEAL (#1)
Bride Protector SEAL (#2)
Montana D-Force (#3)
Cowboy D-Force (#4)
Montana Ranger (#5)
Montana Dog Soldier (#6)
Montana SEAL Daddy (#7)
Montana Ranger's Wedding Vow (#8)
Montana Rescue

MONTANA SEAL DADDY

BROTHERHOOD PROTECTORS BOOK #7

New York Times & *USA Today*
Bestselling Author

ELLE JAMES

ELLE JAMES

MONTANA
SEAL DADDY

BROTHERHOOD PROTECTORS

CHAPTER 1

"I DON'T THINK I'll ever get used to this heat." Daphne Miller sat on the front porch of the small clapboard house out in the middle of the hills in practically nowhere Utah. She fanned herself with a five-month old copy of a celebrity magazine, wishing she were anywhere else in the world. "Do you think they're any closer to getting the evidence they need to nail the bastard who killed Sylvia Jansen? I'd think my testimony alone would be sufficient to put him away for a very long time. Otherwise, why go to all the trouble of witness protection?"

Her forty-seven-year-old bodyguard with the gray streaks at his temples and weathered skin sat in a wooden rocking chair, his feet resting on the porch railing, a piece of straw sticking out of his mouth. Chuck Johnson rolled the straw between his teeth before answering. "You'd think after a year, the feds would have what they need."

Daphne pushed to her feet, restlessness fueling her

irritation. "All I know is that I've sat in this cabin in this godforsaken heat for longer than I can stand. I need to move on with my life. I can't stay here forever. For all we know, they've forgotten I saw anything. Harrison Cooper probably thinks I'm dead or fell off the face of the earth. He might have moved on to his next victim by now. And I'm sitting here doing nothing." She paced to the end of the porch and back, skirting Chuck and his feet propped against the porch railing.

A tiny cry sounded inside the house.

"I'll get her." Chuck dropped his booted feet to the porch and hurried inside to check on Maya, Daphne's three-month old baby girl.

Daphne held up her hands and snorted. "He's even better at parenting than her own mother." She loved Maya, but sometimes she wondered if Maya loved Chuck more than her.

Chuck returned to the porch carrying Maya on one arm, cradling the back of her head with his opposite hand. He handed the child to Daphne. "I changed her, but it's not a dirty diaper that's making her fussy. She's hungry."

Daphne took the baby in her arms, sank into the rocking chair and lifted the hem of her tank top.

Too hot for a bra, she'd left it off that morning, giving Maya free access to her milk supply.

The baby rooted around until she found Daphne's nipple and sucked hungrily, making slurping noises that made Daphne laugh.

Chuck cleared his throat and turned away. "I'll make some iced tea."

"Thank you." Daphne smiled at the man's reluctance to watch the baby nursing. Hell, he'd been there when Maya was born and helped Daphne when she'd had trouble getting the baby to latch on. Why he would feel the need to give her privacy now was a mystery. But Daphne liked to push his buttons. Anything for a reaction in the incredible boredom of her current situation.

Short of feeding Maya, Chuck did everything else with the baby, including getting down on the floor to play with her when Daphne was too tired to entertain her sweet baby girl.

How she wished things had turned out differently. But then she'd wished that for the past year. Not the part about being pregnant or having a baby. Maya was the light of her life. What Daphne despised was being stuck in this godforsaken corner of the Utah desert hill country with nothing to do but count the minutes of every day. If something didn't happen soon, she'd explode.

She switched Maya to the other breast and let the baby drink her fill. The day was much like every other day. Wake up to feed Maya, change her diaper, cook breakfast for herself and Chuck and, sometimes, one of the other guards. The sun rose, the sun set and on and on and on... Only the occasional rare, violent storm ever broke their routine. God, how she wished for one now.

Daphne leaned Maya up on her shoulder and patted the bubbles out of her tummy. She cradled the baby in the curve of her arm and then sat in the growing heat, wondering where she'd gone wrong in her life to deserve so much drama and yet so much boredom.

Chuck emerged through the back screen door and took up his position in the rocking chair. For all intents and purposes, he appeared to be relaxed and enjoying the suffocating heat of the late fall day.

Daphne sighed and rocked Maya in her arms. "I'll be glad when winter finally gets here."

"You and me both," Chuck said, his gaze on the horizon and his voice even.

"Tell me again about what you did for the Navy SEALs," Daphne coaxed.

In profile, he arched an eyebrow. "I already told you a dozen times. Aren't you tired of my stories?"

She shrugged. "Beats boredom. And it gives me an idea of what Maya's father might be doing right now, as we speak."

Chuck sighed. "There's nothing sexy about tromping through the desert, carrying all of your equipment on your back, steel plates in your vest and facing an enemy that uses women and children as shields to block the bullets meant for them."

Daphne stared down at Maya, her heart contracting. She couldn't imagine someone putting a bullet through her baby girl's chest. "Then tell me about your training to become a SEAL." She liked hearing about the rigors of BUD/S training, and how only the best of the best made it through to the end.

Chuck had survived BUD/S training. Since Brandon had made it through as well, he was another man who'd proved he was one of the best.

Again, Chuck sighed and started at the beginning of

his training and told her of the different weeks and what each entailed.

Daphne half-listened...and half-daydreamed about meeting Maya's father in Cozumel.

She'd been there on what should have been her honeymoon, but had turned out to be a solitary vacation. She'd gone with a heavy heart, having lost her fiancé six months earlier to a brain tumor. Because they'd had non-refundable tickets, Jonah had insisted she go, even though it would be without him.

During his treatment and decline, Daphne had been at his side. He'd insisted she go as part of her promise to move on, find love, get married and have children.

At the time of Jonah's death, Daphne was convinced she'd never find another man to love as much as she'd loved Jonah. He'd been her everything, from the moment they'd met in high school, through college and during his final hours on earth.

He'd loved her unconditionally and had wanted half-a-dozen children with her, the little house with the white picket fence and everything normal couples dreamed of when making plans for their futures.

Two months after he'd proposed to her, he'd fallen ill. After many tests, X-rays, scans and MRIs, the diagnosis had been grim. He had terminal brain cancer and less than five months to live.

All of their plans were pushed to the side as they fought to change that diagnosis to something that involved growing old together.

Alas, nearly five months sped by, and no amount of

medication slowed the growth of the tumor. At four months, three weeks and two days following his diagnosis, Jonah slipped into a coma and died in Daphne's arms.

Before he passed, he'd made her promise to go on their honeymoon and find a man who made her heart beat faster. A man who would love her always and provide her with the family she and Jonah had always wanted. And he'd asked her to name a little girl after their honeymoon resort in remembrance of the love Daphne and Jonah had shared in his short time on earth.

Daphne stared down at the baby girl in her arms.

Maya with her black curls, so unlike Daphne's straight blond hair. Jonah had had light brown hair and blue eyes. Nothing about Maya reminded Daphne of Jonah, except her name.

Even then, she reminded Daphne more of the man she'd met in Cozumel, her baby's father, a tall, dark, handsome Navy SEAL who'd found her sitting on the beach one night, alone and crying.

Brandon Rayne, or Boomer, as his teammates had nicknamed him, could have walked away, leaving the weepy woman on the sand in the moonlight, but he hadn't. He'd dropped down beside her, taken her hand, pulled her into his arms and held her until her tears stopped falling.

He'd listened to her sad story, patted her back and held her. When she'd wiped away the tears and collected herself, he'd stood, held out a hand and pulled her up into his arms and kissed her forehead. "Everything is going to be all right," he'd assured her.

She stared up into his moonlit dark eyes. "How do you know?"

He chuckled. "I don't. But being on a sandy beach with a beautiful woman makes me wholly optimistic." Then he'd walked her back to her room at the resort and given her his cell phone number in case she ever wanted to walk on the beach at night. He didn't like the idea of her walking alone.

And that's how their brief and fiery romance spun up into a raging flame. If Daphne believed in ghosts, she'd bet Jonah had sent the SEAL to remind her that her fiancé had died, not her. She had a life to live, and oh, by the way, this handsome SEAL seemed interested in her and wanted to spend time with her.

Once she got over the guilt, Daphne enjoyed the quiet walks at night on the beach. And what was moonlight without a kiss?

One kiss with Boomer wasn't nearly enough. By the second night, he'd invited her to dance and then to his bungalow for a drink. The remaining five days were spent together in paradise. Swimming, dancing, parasailing and learning how to love as if for the first time.

When the last night came, Daphne slipped out of his room, after he fell asleep to return to hers to pack for the trip home. She hadn't wanted to wake him, hating tearful goodbyes. She wanted to remember him as he was, big, gorgeous and naked against the sheets.

On her way from his bungalow to her room in the tower, she'd run across a young man, arguing with a woman.

The woman slapped the young man.

Daphne had been too far away to hear what she said, but clearly, she wasn't happy with the man. When the woman turned to walk away, the blond man clasped her wrist and spun her toward him.

She told him to let go.

When he didn't, she tugged hard, trying to free herself.

Daphne had sped up, trying to get closer to help the woman.

By the time she reached them, the blond man had wrapped his hands around the woman's neck so tightly, he was choking her.

The woman beat at his chest with her fists, but he wouldn't release his grip.

Daphne grabbed a stick from the ground and hit the man over and over, but he wouldn't let go of the woman until her body sagged and fell to the ground.

Then he turned his attention to Daphne.

The man blocked the path, preventing her from running back to the bungalow where Boomer lay sleeping peacefully.

With no other choice, Daphne spun and ran toward the resort, the sound of footsteps pounding on the path behind her. She'd almost reached the entrance when an arm reached out of the darkness, grabbed her, yanked her into the shadow of the bushes, and pushed her toward the ground. A hand clamped over her mouth, muffling her attempt to scream.

"Be still, or he'll find you and kill you," a voice whispered into her ear.

Steps crunched on the gravel path, heading her direction.

Daphne lay still, more afraid of the man who'd choked a woman to death than the stranger holding her in the darkness.

The killer stalked past her, his eyes narrow, his gaze darting into the shadows. In his left hand, he held a small handgun.

Freezing in place, Daphne held her breath, praying he didn't see her lying there. Vulnerable to the man holding her and to the killer brandishing a gun, she prayed she'd chosen the lesser of two evils.

The assailant tucked the weapon into waistband of his trousers and closed his suit jacket over the bulge, before entering the resort tower.

Not until the door closed behind him, did Daphne let go of the breath she'd held.

The man holding her removed his hand from her mouth and loosened the arm around her middle.

She scrambled to her feet and stared at the stranger as he pushed to his feet and stood. He towered over her, his muscular body even more proof he could have had his way with her and she'd have had little chance of fighting free.

That's how she remembered meeting Chuck.

He'd been the one responsible for saving her life and that of her unborn baby by whisking her away from Cozumel and back to the States.

"I'm Agent Johnson. Chuck Johnson." He'd shown her his credentials as a DEA agent in pursuit of a man who smuggled drugs and murdered beautiful women.

"That man chasing you happens to be the son of a high-powered senator. He's suspected of drug and human trafficking, as well as several counts of murder."

"Then why aren't you stopping him?" Daphne demanded.

"He's a slippery bastard. The witnesses or drug dealers have a habit of turning up dead before charges can be brought against him." The stranger frowned. "Why was he chasing you?"

Daphne's heart plummeted into her belly as she recalled how hard the woman had fought and how many times Daphne had hit the man with the stick to no avail. "He killed a woman."

"Show me." Chuck edged up to the path, glancing both ways before motioning for her to go ahead of him.

Before they reached the point at which the woman had been strangled, two men appeared from the direction of the beach, dressed in black. The glow of the Tiki lamps lighting the path glinted off the smooth metal of the pistols they carried in their hands.

Chuck pulled her back into the shadows and blocked her body with his.

But he didn't block her entire vision.

The two men in black moved the woman's body, carrying it toward the ocean.

"See what I mean?" her muscular rescuer said. "He has a cleanup detail following him around."

Shocked at what she'd just seen, Daphne tried to push him aside. "You can't let him get away with killing someone."

"And what do you suggest? If I kill those men, it will

appear as if I killed the woman. You and I will be split up, and more cleanup crews will be called in to deal with you and me. Our best bet is to get you out of here before they come looking for you."

At that exact moment, two more men appeared, coming from the direction of the resort, also dressed in black and carrying weapons.

Daphne sank back into the bushes, shaking. "I know the man staying in the fourth bungalow from the end of the path. We can hide there," she suggested.

Chuck shook his head. "No good. If you were there before, they'll track you down to that location again. The staff knows the comings and goings of all the guests. And they can be bribed."

But Daphne wanted to go back to where she'd left Boomer sleeping. If she'd stayed with him the entire night, she wouldn't be in this predicament. The woman would still be dead, but Daphne wouldn't now be targeted for elimination.

Again, she stayed still, waiting for the two men in black to pass by their position. She had no other choice in the matter. She had to get away from the scene of the crime. Perhaps then, they could circle back and report the crime to the local authorities.

That had been a year ago.

As far as Daphne knew, Harrison Cooper was still free, while she and Maya had been stuck in a cabin in Utah, waiting for something to happen that would put Cooper behind bars.

When Chuck paused in his description of Hell Week at BUD/S, Daphne pushed to her feet. "I'm going to go put Maya to bed. Hold that thought. I want to hear more." She smiled at the only human contact she'd had besides the doctors and nurses who'd delivered her baby in the Salt Lake City hospital and her two-man protection crew who guarded the entrance to this lonely house.

Chuck had admitted he wasn't with the DEA. He was with a super-secret government entity, assigned to clean up corruption amongst politicians. He'd come up with false identification and insurance cards to cover her and the baby. As soon as she was able, he'd packed up her and Maya and orchestrated their disappearance from the hospital into the foothills of Utah's Wasatch Mountain Range, near the Wyoming border.

Daphne had grown to love Chuck like a surrogate father or a favorite big brother. On more than one occasion, she found herself referring to him as Maya's godfather. And he was her only link to the outside world.

He had connections with the SEAL community, having retired from the Navy before taking on a role with the DEA.

Daphne knew, if she asked, he'd tell her where Boomer was, and whether he was dead or alive. When she'd been at her lowest, suffering from postpartum depression shortly after Maya was born, he'd told her Boomer was back in the States, preparing to deploy to Iraq.

She'd been tempted to reach out to Boomer and let him know he had a beautiful baby girl. But how fair would that have been, knowing he was about to deploy.

And by letting him know about his baby, she might give up her location, something she couldn't afford to do. Her life wasn't nearly as important to her as keeping Maya safe.

Now that she had a baby, she had to do everything in her power to protect Maya from Harrison Cooper's cleanup team. As effective as they'd been in Cozumel, they would show no remorse over using an infant as a bargaining chip to lure Daphne out into the open. Once they located her, she'd disappear, and then they'd have no use for Maya.

Daphne's heart squeezed hard in her chest as she laid her baby in the crib.

Maya's sweet lips puckered as if she were still suckling at Daphne's breast. She squirmed, stretched and laid still, her belly full, her comfort secured.

Daphne smiled and straightened, her attention drawn to the window overlooking the dirt road leading up to the cabin. A plume of dust rose from a vehicle moving swiftly up the mile-long track.

A second of concern rippled through Daphne, but she refused to be alarmed. Not yet.

Their dayshift gate guard, Rodney Smith, was one of two men who'd been assigned to provide backup and support. Rodney was on day shift, while Paul Caney preferred nights and slept in town during the day. They stood guard at the entrance gate to the mountain cabin a mile away, keeping in contact with Chuck via hand-held, two-way radios.

"Chuck? Has Rodney checked in?" she called out.

Chuck entered the house, passed the door to Maya's

nursery and exited through the front door onto the porch. With the two-way radio held to his ear, his gaze fixed on the cloud of dust racing toward them. "Smith, report," he said over and over.

When nothing but static came across the radio, Chuck spun and raced back into the house, his face stern, his fists clenched. "Take Maya to the shed. Now! This isn't a drill."

Daphne's heart tripped and raced. They'd practiced this drill numerous times. If Chuck said take Maya to the shed, they were in trouble.

Daphne reached for her "go pack", the backpack carrying the essentials necessary for the baby, slung it over her shoulders, then she gathered Maya into her arms and ran out the back of the house to the shed.

In the shed, she pulled a baby sling over her shoulder, settled Maya into the sling and tightened it so that she fit snugly against Daphne's chest. She settled a helmet over her head and buckled the strap.

Chuck arrived a few seconds later and flung open the back doors he'd installed on the shed.

"Everything set?" Daphne asked as she swung her leg over the seat of a four-wheeler.

He nodded. "Do you want me to take Maya?"

Daphne shook her head. "I've got her."

"You can take the lead until we reach the pass. I've got your six. The paths are narrow. The vehicles coming up the road won't be able to follow for long—if they make it past the surprise I left for them."

"Where will we go?" Daphne asked.

"I have a friend in Montana. He'll know what to do. He'll help protect you and Maya."

Daphne nodded, pressed the throttle lever on the four-wheeler and sent the vehicle lurching forward and up the trail into the mountains.

Chuck followed, bringing up the rear, armed to the teeth with rifles, handguns, knives and hand grenades.

All they had to do was get far enough away from rifle fire, and they'd make good their escape from those attacking the cabin. But the race up the side of the mountain left them exposed for several minutes. What they needed was a distraction.

Daphne didn't look back, she held tightly to the handlebars of the ATV, moving as quickly as she could up the rough mountain trail, praying the men heading for the cabin didn't stop and take aim at the riders on the escaping four-wheelers.

An explosion echoed off the hillsides, followed by another, even bigger, that ripped through the air, shaking the earth beneath the four, knobby tires. Daphne nearly lost her grip on the four-wheeler handlebars. She risked a quick glance over her shoulder at the cabin. Nothing remained of her temporary home. Nothing but debris, fire and smoke.

Chuck slowed, frowning. "I planned on the first explosion, but not the second."

"Did you detonate the house?" Daphne asked.

Her protector shook his head. "No. I had some trip wires set up in front of the house. Looks like it just made them mad enough to destroy the house."

Daphne swallowed the sob rising up her throat,

threatening to choke off her air. That cabin had been her baby's first home. The crib, the extra clothing and toys had been all Maya had known. Where they'd go from here was a huge unknown.

All Daphne knew was she had to get Maya to safety. Everything that had been in the cabin was just *stuff*. She could replace stuff. She couldn't replace the life of her baby girl.

Chuck had a friend in Montana.

After a year, waiting for something to happen and thinking it never would, Daphne was now a believer. Her heart weighed heavily for the guard on the gate. More than likely, Rodney was dead.

She prayed Chuck's friend in Montana had the power and resources to protect her and Maya.

ABOUT THE AUTHOR

ELLE JAMES also writing as MYLA JACKSON is a *New York Times* and *USA Today* Bestselling author of books including cowboys, intrigues and paranormal adventures that keep her readers on the edges of their seats. When she's not at her computer, she's traveling, snow skiing, boating, or riding her ATV, dreaming up new stories. Learn more about Elle James at www.elle-james.com

Website | Facebook | Twitter | GoodReads | Newsletter | BookBub | Amazon

Or visit her alter ego Myla Jackson at mylajackson.com
Website | Facebook | Twitter | Newsletter

Follow Me!
www.ellejames.com
ellejames@ellejames.com

ALSO BY ELLE JAMES

Montana Rescue (Sleeper SEAL)

Hot SEAL Salty Dog (SEALs in Paradise)

Hot SEAL Hawaiian Nights (SEALs in Paradise)

Hot SEAL Bachelor Party (SEALs in Paradise)

Brotherhood Protectors Vol 1

Hellfire Series

Hellfire, Texas (#1)

Justice Burning (#2)

Smoldering Desire (#3)

Hellfire in High Heels (#4)

Playing With Fire (#5)

Up in Flames (#6)

Total Meltdown (#7)

Declan's Defenders

Marine Force Recon (#1)

Show of Force (#2)

Full Force (#3)

Driving Force (#4)

Tactical Force (#5)

Disruptive Force (#6)

Mission: Six

One Intrepid SEAL

Two Dauntless Hearts

Three Courageous Words

Four Relentless Days

Five Ways to Surrender

Six Minutes to Midnight

Hearts & Heroes Series

Wyatt's War (#1)

Mack's Witness (#2)

Ronin's Return (#3)

Sam's Surrender (#4)

Take No Prisoners Series

SEAL's Honor (#1)

SEAL'S Desire (#2)

SEAL's Embrace (#3)

SEAL's Obsession (#4)

SEAL's Proposal (#5)

SEAL's Seduction (#6)

SEAL'S Defiance (#7)

SEAL's Deception (#8)

SEAL's Deliverance (#9)

SEAL's Ultimate Challenge (#10)

Texas Billionaire Club

Tarzan & Janine (#1)

Something To Talk About (#2)

Who's Your Daddy (#3)

Love & War (#4)

Ballistic Cowboy

Hot Combat (#1)

Hot Target (#2)

Hot Zone (#3)

Hot Velocity (#4)

Cajun Magic Mystery Series

Voodoo on the Bayou (#1)

Voodoo for Two (#2)

Deja Voodoo (#3)

Cajun Magic Mysteries Books 1-3

Billionaire Online Dating Service

The Billionaire Husband Test (#1)

The Billionaire Cinderella Test (#2)

The Billionaire Bride Test (#3)

The Billionaire Daddy Test (#4)

The Billionaire Matchmaker Test (#5)

SEAL Of My Own

Navy SEAL Survival

Navy SEAL Captive

Navy SEAL To Die For

Navy SEAL Six Pack

Devil's Shroud Series

Deadly Reckoning (#1)

Deadly Engagement (#2)

Deadly Liaisons (#3)

Deadly Allure (#4)

Deadly Obsession (#5)

Deadly Fall (#6)

Covert Cowboys Inc Series

Triggered (#1)

Taking Aim (#2)

Bodyguard Under Fire (#3)

Cowboy Resurrected (#4)

Navy SEAL Justice (#5)

Navy SEAL Newlywed (#6)

High Country Hideout (#7)

Clandestine Christmas (#8)

Thunder Horse Series

Hostage to Thunder Horse (#1)

Thunder Horse Heritage (#2)

Thunder Horse Redemption (#3)

Christmas at Thunder Horse Ranch (#4)

Demon Series

Hot Demon Nights (#1)

Demon's Embrace (#2)

Tempting the Demon (#3)

Lords of the Underworld

Witch's Initiation (#1)

Witch's Seduction (#2)

Bundle of Trouble

Killer Body

Operation XOXO

An Unexpected Clue

Baby Bling

Under Suspicion, With Child

Texas-Size Secrets

Cowboy Sanctuary

Lakota Baby

Dakota Meltdown

Beneath the Texas Moon

Made in the USA
Las Vegas, NV
28 September 2021